"How long ha~~s~~ ~~____ ____~~ you two have seen each other?" Matthew asked Zoey.

Zoey stiffened, searching for undercurrents of suspicion in the husky voice. Zoey tried to tell herself it only made sense that his concern would be centered on her grandmother now.

But he probably thought that she had shown up, circling like a vulture, to determine just how sick her grandmother was. He'd seen the condition of her Jeep. The clothing piled in the backseat. More than likely she was down on her luck. Looking for someone to take care of her.

The thought turned Zoey's stomach.

She wouldn't try to explain that the reason she'd come back was to give, not take.

It wouldn't make any difference. As soon as he left, the good pastor would no doubt ask around town—find at least a dozen people who would cheerfully supply all the gruesome details of her past—and he wouldn't believe her anyway.

Books by Kathryn Springer

Love Inspired

Tested by Fire
Her Christmas Wish
By Her Side
For Her Son's Love
A Treasure Worth Keeping
Hidden Treasures
Family Treasures
Jingle Bell Babies
*A Place to Call Home
*Love Finds a Home
*The Prodigal Comes Home

*Mirror Lake

Steeple Hill

Front Porch Princess
Hearts Evergreen
  "A Match Made for Christmas"
Picket Fence Promises
The Prince Charming List

KATHRYN SPRINGER

is a lifelong Wisconsin resident. Growing up in a "newspaper" family, she spent long hours as a child plunking out stories on her mother's typewriter and hasn't stopped writing since! She loves to write inspirational romance because it allows her to combine her faith in God with her love of a happy ending.

The Prodigal Comes Home
Kathryn Springer

Steeple
Hill®

Published by Steeple Hill Books™

STEEPLE HILL BOOKS

Steeple
Hill®

Recycling programs
for this product may
not exist in your area.

ISBN-13: 978-0-373-81528-9

THE PRODIGAL COMES HOME

www.SteepleHill.com

Printed in U.S.A.

"He put a new song in my mouth,
a hymn of praise to our God.
Many will see and fear
and put their trust in the Lord."
—*Psalms* 40:3

Chapter One

She shouldn't have come back.

The thought raced through Zoey Decker's mind the moment she spotted a square, unassuming green road sign sprouting from the snow-covered ditch.

Mirror Lake—3 miles.

Spots began to dance in front of her eyes and she stomped on the brake, wrestling the Jeep onto the side of the road. Maybe she should get out of the vehicle for a few minutes. Stretch her legs.

A bracing March wind pinched Zoey's cheeks as she bailed awkwardly out of the driver's seat and started down the road, fatigue adding weight to her limbs.

For the past few hours, she'd been telling herself that she'd made the right decision. Now—only a few minutes from her destination—she was having second thoughts.

Zoey's gaze locked on the sign again.

What was that old saying?

You can't go home again?

But Mirror Lake had never been *home*. Not really. It just happened to be the town where her grandparents had retired. The place her parents had dumped her off because they didn't know how to deal with a full-blown case of teenage rebellion.

And even though Zoey had only lived in Mirror Lake two short years—which must have seemed more like a lifetime to her sixty-five-year-old grandparents—she had definitely made her mark.

A *black* one…

"Are you lost?"

Zoey whirled around at the sound of a voice behind her. A low, masculine rumble that had her questioning her impulsive decision to stop on a quiet stretch of road sandwiched between two imposing walls of towering white pine.

With not a house in sight.

She hadn't expected to see anyone. Not this early in the morning. And especially not a man, who'd materialized seemingly out of nowhere.

Zoey caught her lower lip between her teeth as she considered the six-foot-tall obstacle that now stood between her and the safety of the Jeep. Chiseled features, tousled dark-blond hair. The lean but muscular frame of someone who probably earned his living outdoors.

Under ordinary circumstances, someone of his size shouldn't have been able to sneak up and catch her unaware—but then again, nothing about the last twenty-four hours had been ordinary. Zoey had spent most of the night navigating miles of national forest, where white-tailed deer far outnumbered the population of the towns she'd driven through.

The guy didn't *look* like a criminal. But how was a woman supposed to know who she could and couldn't trust these days? And if Zoey was completely honest, she knew her track record in that department hadn't always been the best.

He shifted his stance, a subtle movement that positioned him closer to the vehicle.

Had the action been deliberate?

Zoey suppressed a shiver and rolled her hands up in the hem of the oversized, hand-knit sweater that had been a gift from her grandmother many Christmases ago.

The man noticed the gesture and his eyebrows dipped together in a frown. "Are you lost?" he repeated.

In a different situation, the question might have made Zoey smile. "It depends on who you ask."

The frown deepened. He obviously didn't understand her wry sense of humor. "Is something wrong with your car?"

"No." At least, Zoey silently amended, nothing that could be fixed on the side of the road. She cast a fond look at the eggplant-purple Jeep, decorated with its contrasting pattern of rust, intricate as a henna tattoo. It had outlived its warranty by at least a few thousand miles and yet somehow managed to get her from Point A to B. That was good enough for her. "I'm fine. My car is fine, too."

Zoey inched forward, silently gauging the distance between them and the vehicle.

He was closer.

"That's good to know." The corners of the man's lips kicked up into a smile and, stranger or not, Zoey could feel her heart doing an impromptu tap dance in her chest. Which only proved she could use a few hours of uninterrupted sleep. "I was out for a run and saw your car parked by the side of the road. I just wanted to make sure everything was okay."

A good Samaritan.

Now Zoey noticed a detail she'd missed the first time. *When you were staring at his face.* He wore a standard runner's uniform. Black sweatpants, a fleece-lined sweatshirt with a faded college logo across the front and tennis shoes.

"I appreciate your concern." *However misplaced.* "But I just needed to get out and…stretch my legs for a minute."

Stretch her legs. Gather her courage. Postpone the inevitable.

All one and the same.

"Stretch your legs." The thread of doubt in the husky voice made Zoey wince.

Right. Most people would have probably chosen to do that at a rest area or gas station. A place with *heat.*

"That's right." Zoey lifted her chin. "Now, if you'll excuse me…" She took another step closer to the Jeep.

So did he.

Zoey's breath hitched in her throat, but all he did was reach out to open the car door for her. And then went still.

Obviously much more observant than she was, he'd immediately spotted the mound of clothing, which happened to be the entire contents of Zoey's closet, along with an eclectic jumble of her earthly possessions heaped onto the backseat. All evidence of the haste in which she'd left the night before.

To make matters worse, Zoey's stomach decided to remind her—quite loudly—that it had been more than twelve hours since she'd eaten. She could have grabbed a snack at some point along the way, but she decided that nothing in the deli case of a gas station would peacefully coexist with the butterflies that had taken up residence in her stomach.

A blush added another layer of color to her already-pink cheeks as the man's gaze cut back to her. His eyes, a warm palette of green and brown that brought back memories of summer walks through the woods, searched hers. Looking for…something.

Afraid of what he might find there, Zoey looked away.

"There's a cafe in town. It's called the Grapevine," he said after a moment. "Could I buy you a cup of coffee? Maybe some breakfast?"

Disappointment arrowed through her. She should have known better. "Does that line usually work?"

"No..." He caught himself. "I mean, no, it isn't a *line*. It's an...offer." His gaze dropped to her hands, still balled up in the bright cocoon of her sweater, before flickering over the mountain of clothing once again. "I'm not even inviting myself along. It would be my treat."

Zoey frowned a little.

He was offering to pay for her breakfast? That didn't make any sense...

Yes, it did.

He thought she was down on her luck, like a stray kitten who needed food and shelter from the cold.

Zoey stifled a groan as she tried to see herself through his eyes. She hadn't bothered to change clothes after her evening performance at the dinner theater where she worked, but he wouldn't know that what she wore was a *costume*. All he would see were paisley-patterned tights peeking through the slashed knees of her faded jeans. Pink canvas tennis shoes, meant for summer instead of snow. A misshapen patchwork sweater that had definitely seen better days.

And Zoey wasn't even going to *think* about what her hair looked like.

Mortified, she slipped past him and dove into the driver's seat. "No thanks, but I appreciate the offer. Really."

He stepped back as Zoey pulled the door shut and

turned the key in the ignition, hoping the temperamental engine would start. It did, after a brief but grating shudder of protest.

When she finally gathered the courage to glance in the rearview mirror, the man was standing in the exact spot where she'd left him.

Watching her drive away.

"You have to actually drink the coffee, not stare at it, in order for the caffeine to kick in, Pastor."

Matt Wilde glanced up and saw Kate Nichols, the owner of the Grapevine cafe, standing next to the booth, armed with a coffee pot. He flashed a rueful smile in her direction. "Sorry. I was somewhere else."

"It must have been somewhere pretty far away," Kate observed. "Usually you're on your third cup by now."

Not so far away, Matt thought. In fact, just a few miles from town.

Corduroy Road had been part of his regular route for over a year. It was a quiet back road that looped around the east side of Mirror Lake. He could have run it blindfolded. And other than the squirrels and birds that chattered at him from the trees, he usually had it all to himself.

Until this morning, when he'd rounded the corner and saw a purple Jeep parked at an angle alongside the road. One look at the rust creeping around the wheel wells and over the bumper like a bad rash and Matt guessed it had broken down.

Then he saw *her*.

A slight figure marching up and down the road, head bent against the wind. The baggy sweater she wore a kaleidoscope of color against a backdrop of gray and white.

Matt had assumed she was a teenager. Until she turned around.

Dark curls framed a face made up small, sharp angles. Her eyes, which by all rights should have been brown, were a pearl gray that reminded him of the lake just before dawn. A dusting of freckles across her nose made her beauty more winsome than exotic.

He hadn't been able to put her out of his mind.

Maybe because you bungled things so badly?

Matt couldn't dismiss the inner voice. Not when it was right.

First he'd startled her. Then he'd insulted her.

He closed his eyes briefly, the memory sawing at his conscience. Instead of understanding that his impulsive offer to buy her breakfast stemmed from compassion, she'd thought he was hitting on her. Hence the hasty departure. The rusty Jeep had lurched forward, the loose tailpipe belching exhaust as she drove away...

"Hey! You left again." Kate waved the order pad in front of his face, amusement sparkling in her eyes. "Your breakfast is coming right up, by the way."

"I didn't order breakfast."

"It's the most important meal of the day." Kate topped off his cup and flitted away.

Matt couldn't summon a smile even though it was a standing joke between them. He would come into the Grapevine and order coffee before going to the church. Kate would return with a plate weighted down with her famous "Lumberjack Special," a mountain of hash browns topped with scrambled eggs and sausage, surrounded by a moat of maple syrup tapped from a local sugar bush.

When she deposited the plate in front of him a few minutes later, Matt shook his head. "No wonder I have to run five miles."

Kate grinned. "Enjoy."

As he ate he thought about this crazy insistence on feeding him that his church members had. Everyone joined in. His congregation at Church of the Pines thought that his bachelor status meant he didn't know how to fry an egg.

He did, but he never turned down a dinner invitation. Jesus frequently went to peoples' homes and built relationships around a table. Matt saw no reason not to follow his Savior's lead.

A blast of cold air rolled into the cafe as the door swung open. Matt's head jerked up. Maybe the woman on the road had decided to take him up on his offer... and give him an opportunity to apologize. But instead of a waif-like young woman with enormous gray eyes, he saw Harold Dinsman, one of Kate's regulars, shuffling toward the row of vinyl-covered stools to stake his claim at the old-fashioned soda counter.

"Is there something wrong with your breakfast this morning, Pastor?" Kate stood next to the booth again, staring down at the plate of food he'd barely made a dent in.

"Not a thing. I just decided to surrender earlier than I usually do." Matt waved a white paper napkin in the air to prove it.

Kate fished the bill out of her apron pocket and handed it to him. "Are you heading over to the church now?"

"Not yet. I'm going to stop by Liz Decker's house and check on her. She sounded tired when we talked last night."

Kate began to collect the dishes. "I heard she was released from the hospital yesterday. How is she?"

"Stubborn." Affection for the older woman, one of Church of the Pines most beloved members, curved Matt's lips into a smile.

"That's what everyone loves about her." Kate smiled back. "So far, she's been refusing to allow some of us to bring in meals or clean her house because she doesn't want anyone to 'fuss' over her. I hope she changes her mind. She's supposed to be taking it easy."

"And that's what I plan to talk to her about." Matt glanced at the bill and thumbed through his wallet. "Pray for me."

Kate chuckled. "With no family in the area, Liz

is going to have to let her church family help out. She's the first one to show up when someone else is in need."

In the year and a half that Matt had known Liz Decker, he'd certainly found that to be true. Her husband, Jonathan, had passed away from a heart attack before Matt moved to Mirror Lake but she continued to remain active in the church. Not only was Liz the choir director, but she had also volunteered to serve on the search committee the congregation had formed to interview prospective candidates after their former pastor retired.

Unfortunately, the members of that committee had quickly discovered that a church with an average attendance of less than a hundred, located in a small town surrounded by thousands of acres of national forest, didn't draw a lot of interest, no matter how charming and picturesque. The congregation finally agreed to send out letters of inquiry to several seminaries, hoping to hire a recent graduate to serve as an interim pastor until Church of the Pines found someone who met their requirements.

Matt, with the ink still wet on his diploma and needing the experience, had applied. Liz Decker had been the one who called and offered him the position. Matt had looked at the opportunity to serve as pastor as more than a temporary position—it had been an affirmation. A sign that God had a place and a purpose for him during the times of doubt when

Matt wondered if the emotional fallout from a failed relationship hadn't ruined his chances for both.

At the end of the summer, the elders had asked if he would consider staying on. So far, Matt hadn't regretted his decision. He'd fallen in the love with the area—and its close-knit community—almost immediately.

The entire congregation had gone out of their way to make him feel at home, especially Liz. The woman had become a combination cheerleader, surrogate grandmother and spiritual advisor, offering plates of homemade treats as often as she offered encouraging passages of scripture.

Matt welcomed the opportunity to take care of her for a change.

"Give Liz my love and remind her that tomorrow is pecan pie day. I'll drop off a piece on my way home from work," Kate said before turning her attention to a family settling into the next booth.

"Will do." Matt shrugged his coat on as an image of the young woman by the road flashed through his mind again.

She hadn't even been wearing a coat. Or boots, for that matter. Winter hadn't released its grip on the north woods yet.

Locals knew not to pack away their cold-weather clothes until at least the middle of June.

Unsettled once again by the memory of that unexpected encounter, Matt's gaze swept over the cars parked on Main Street.

Not a purple Jeep in sight.

But even though he couldn't see her, Matt knew that God could.

Lord, I don't know her story. I don't know who she is or where she's going, but you do. Please look out for her. If she doesn't know you, put people into her path who do...

Chapter Two

Zoey's hands began to tremble as she turned onto
Carriage Street. At the end of the dead-end road stood
a stately Victorian, tucked behind a screen of gnarled
willow trees. Built in the mid-eighteen hundreds, the
house remained a charming but faded monument to
an era when local lumber barons lived and reigned
like royalty.

Most people would have chosen to purchase a
cute little log cabin on the lake, but not Jonathan
and Elizabeth Decker. After her grandfather retired
and Mirror Lake had become their permanent residence rather than a favorite vacation spot, he and
Gran had purchased their "dream" home—an authen-
tic "painted lady," complete with sloping rooflines,
gabled windows and a warren of rooms designed to
hold company.

And rebellious teenage granddaughters.

Memories began to stir. Everything looked the
way Zoey remembered it, as if she were looking at

a photograph. The siding still wore a coat of pale orchid paint, staying true to its original color scheme. The front door remained a welcoming butter yellow; the gingerbread trim was a muted shade of sea foam green.

A flameless taper candle burned in every window, night and day.

Tears banked behind Zoey's eyes as she noticed the ruffled curtains framing the windows in the second-floor turret that overlooked the flower garden. Not only because they still hung there—ten years later— but because she remembered her reaction the first time she'd seen them.

Her grandparents had gone out of their way to make Zoey feel at home when she'd arrived, but bitterness and anger had clouded her vision. She had declared that she was sixteen, not six. She hadn't appreciated the bedroom, which her grandfather had painted a soft, seashell pink in her honor, nor their effort. She didn't belong there, with them, any more than she belonged with her parents. Zoey had known it was only a matter of time before her grandparents figured it out, too.

And she'd be sent away again.

At the time, Zoey decided it might not hurt as much if she hastened the process. The fact that her grandparents had refused to cooperate had made her decision feel even worse.

Blinking back the tears that threatened to spill over, Zoey got out of the Jeep and picked her way up the brick walkway that led to the front door, skirting puddles of melting snow.

Maybe she should have called first. But when her mother had contacted her with the news that Gran had just spent a week in the hospital with complications caused by pneumonia, all Zoey could think about was being there for the woman who had once been there for her.

Even if she hadn't appreciated it at the time.

Gathering up her courage, Zoey tapped her knuckles against the ornate wooden door. A few seconds later, she heard the thump of footsteps across the hardwood floor in the foyer. They were too heavy to be Gran's, but her grandfather had been gone for several years now.

Guilt caused the knot in Zoey's throat to swell. She hadn't come back to Mirror Lake to attend Grandpa Jonathan's funeral. It would have meant facing her parents—and her past—and Zoey hadn't been ready. She'd sent a bouquet of flowers instead. And even though she hadn't signed the card, she'd hoped her grandmother would know who they were from.

The door opened and Zoey could only stare in disbelief at the person on the other side.

It was *him.*

The man from the road.

Matt, who had come to the door ready to intercept yet another tuna casserole or pan of lemon bars meant for Liz, felt his heart drop to his feet when he saw who was standing on the front stoop. A woman whose features had already become imprinted in his memory.

The heart-shaped face framed by glossy dark curls. Wary gray eyes that seemed to change like the surface of the lake. The intriguing constellation of chocolate-colored freckles scattered across the bridge of her nose.

Matt blinked but she didn't disappear. And she looked equally as stunned—and confused—to see him.

"I…I'm sorry." She started to back away.

No matter what had brought her here, Matt wasn't about to lose her again.

"Please, come in for a minute." He gave her what he hoped was a reassuring smile. "This time of the year, it's important to keep the hot separate from the cold."

And he couldn't help but notice that she still wasn't wearing a coat.

She wavered for a moment and then slipped into the foyer. Matt closed the door.

"Now, how can I help you?" He instantly regretted the question when color bloomed in her cheeks, as if she were remembering this wasn't the first time he'd offered his assistance.

She caught her lower lip between her teeth. "I'm looking for Elizabeth Decker. Does she still…live here?"

In spite of Matt's initial amazement that the woman

he hadn't been able to stop thinking about was actually there—right in front of him—warning bells began to go off in his head. As long as he'd known Liz, Matt had never heard anyone refer to her as "Elizabeth." And the fact that the woman from the road wasn't even sure she had the right address didn't exactly put his mind at ease, either.

Liz Decker's reputation for compassion—and generosity—was widely known in the area. Matt wasn't naive. For every person like Liz, there was always someone willing to take advantage of their kind-hearted nature.

He prayed the woman standing next to him wasn't one of them, but given the fragile state of Liz's health, he couldn't take any chances.

"Yes, Mrs. Decker lives here, but she is resting at the moment. I'll tell her you stopped by, Ms.…." Matt deliberately let his voice trail off, waiting for her to fill in the blank.

"Zoey."

But it wasn't the woman standing in front of him who supplied her name.

Matt spun around and saw Liz standing—no, teetering was more like it—in the arched doorway of the parlor, one hand pressed against her chest and the other groping for something to hold on to.

The change in her was alarming. Five minutes ago, they had been sharing a pot of coffee and a plate of cinnamon rolls while Liz, one of those rare people who could find the humor in any situation, entertained him with stories of what Matt guessed had been, in fact, an exhausting weeklong stay in the hospital.

He was at Liz's side in a heartbeat, tucking her arm through his as she sagged against him.

"I think you better sit down," he murmured. But his attempt to guide her gently back into the parlor was met with unexpected resistance.

"I'm fine," Liz gasped, making a feeble attempt to shake him off.

"Gran...I'm so sorry. Are you all right?"

Two thoughts collided in Matt's mind. The woman—*Zoey*—had followed him down the hall. And she'd just called Liz "Gran."

His gaze bounced back and forth between the two. Both women had the chalk-like pallor and dazed expressions of victims from an accident scene.

"Okay, I have another idea. Let's *all* sit down." To Matt's surprise, the young woman took Liz's other arm. Together they shepherded her toward the comfortable settee in front of the fireplace. Once Liz was settled against the cushions, Matt poured a glass of water from the pitcher on the coffee table and handed it to her.

"Thank you."

To his relief, the cracks in Liz's voice had mended and she sounded more like herself. Her color began to return, too, although she still wore the shell-shocked look of someone who had just received bad news.

And maybe she had.

Matt's gaze flicked to Zoey, who had perched on

the edge of a wingback chair, fingers knotted together in her lap. The mixture of regret and worry simmering in her eyes appeared genuine.

He tried to remember what Liz had told him about her family. He knew she had a son and daughter-in-law on the mission field in Africa, but to his recollection she hadn't said anything about grandchildren. Or, more specifically, a grand*daughter*.

He looked for a physical resemblance between the two but failed to find one. Not only was the color of their hair and eyes different, but Matt was also unable to whittle Liz's soft, rounded features down to the spare, delicate brush strokes that made up Zoey's face.

"I can't believe you're here," Liz said, fumbling with a pair of glasses suspended by two gold chains around her neck.

Zoey ducked her head when Liz put them on, as if she didn't want to give her the opportunity to take a closer look. "I should have called first," she murmured.

Liz dismissed the words instantly. "Don't be silly. The door is always open to friends. And family."

Zoey flinched but Liz didn't seem to notice. She turned to Matt. "This is my granddaughter, Zoey Decker," she said, a radiant smile beginning to bloom on her face now that the initial shock had begun to fade. "Zoey, this is Matthew Wilde. He is one of my very good friends and the pastor at Church of the Pines."

Matt had gotten used to people's initial surprise when they discovered he was a minister. He wasn't sure if their reaction had something to do with the fact that was in his early thirties or because he preferred blue jeans and T-shirts to a suit and tie.

But Zoey Decker didn't look surprised.

She looked horrified.

It was a good thing she was sitting down because Zoey's knees turned to liquid. Again. Especially since she hadn't completely recovered from the shock of seeing *him* open the front door.

"It's nice to meet you, Zoey," Matthew Wilde— *Pastor Wilde*—said quietly.

She managed a jerky nod, wondering if he would mention the fact that they already had met.

As humiliating as their brief encounter had been, Zoey hadn't been able to stop thinking about him. The man knew nothing about her and yet the genuine concern in his eyes when he'd offered to buy her breakfast had touched a chord deep inside of her.

Maybe that's why he was concerned, an inner voice mocked. *Because he doesn't know you. If he did, he would have kept right on going...*

At least Matthew Wilde's erroneous assumption that she could use a free meal had motivated her to stop at the first gas station she saw to seek out a mirror. What she saw there had prompted her to take some time to wash up, finger comb her hair into some resemblance of order and dab on a layer of makeup to hide the circles under her eyes. Zoey had also driven around the lake and stopped to watch the rippling waters before gathering up the courage to return to the house on Carriage Street.

"You didn't drive all night, did you?" Gran leaned forward, in full "hospitality mode" now. "Are you hungry?"

Zoey couldn't look at Matthew Wilde, who probably could have guessed the answer to both questions. "No, I'm—"

The pastor neatly cut her off. "Even if you had breakfast, you can't pass up one of these cinnamon rolls." He transferred one to a plate and handed it to her.

Zoey couldn't refuse without appearing rude. She balanced the plate on one knee, her throat so tight she knew she wouldn't be able to swallow a bite.

"There's coffee left in the carafe…" Liz paused and shook her head. "Listen to me! Do you drink coffee, Zoey, or would you prefer something else?"

"Coffee is fine. Thank you."

Before she could finish the sentence, the pastor had poured her a cup.

Silence swelled and filled in the empty spaces between them. Zoey picked at the edge of the cinnamon roll, if only to give her hands something to do. She could feel the weight of two pairs of eyes.

Suddenly, her grandmother chuckled. "Oh my goodness—that sweater you're wearing! I can't believe you kept it all these years. It was my first project after I joined Esther Redstone's knitting group."

"I love it." Zoey looked down and made a half-hearted attempt to smooth down another one of the loops that had worked its way loose in the wash.

Over the years, the sweater had moved with her when she'd been forced to leave other things behind. It might have become a little misshapen and fuzzy, but Zoey hadn't been able to part with it.

"Your grandpa teased me while I was making it. He said it would be more suited for a man named Joseph than a girl named Zoey. He was right, you know." A smile deepened the creases fanning out from Liz's brown eyes. "I must have used every color of yarn in the shop."

At the mention of her grandfather, Zoey felt that familiar pinch of regret. "I remember."

"How long has it been since you two have seen each other?" Matthew directed the question at Zoey.

She stiffened, searching for undercurrents of suspicion in the husky voice. Zoey tried to tell herself it only made sense that his concern would be centered on her grandmother now.

He *knew* Liz.

But he probably thought that *she* had shown up, circling like a vulture, to determine just how sick her grandmother was. He'd seen the condition of her Jeep. The clothing piled in the backseat. More than likely, he thought she was looking for someone to take care of her.

The idea turned Zoey's stomach.

She wouldn't try to explain that the reason she'd come back was to *give,* not take.

It wouldn't make any difference. As soon as he left, the good pastor would no doubt ask around town—find at least a dozen people who would cheerfully supply all the gruesome details of her past—and he wouldn't believe her anyway.

"Much too long." Gran answered the question, reaching out and giving Zoey's hand a comforting squeeze.

Zoey fought the urge to cling to her. When she'd made the impulsive decision to drive to Mirror Lake and see Gran, she hadn't anticipated the avalanche of feelings her visit would trigger.

She hadn't expected that a place she had lived for two short, unhappy years of her life would feel like coming home.

Like the outside of the house, the inside looked exactly the way she remembered it. Right down to the powder-blue velvet furniture and the collection of porcelain birds decorating the fireplace mantle.

And Gran...she may have added a few more lines, but she was as sweet and warmhearted as Zoey remembered.

Maybe the only thing that had changed was *her.*

Not that Zoey expected anyone—not even her grandmother— to believe it.

"You can stay for lunch, can't you? Or are you just passing through Mirror Lake?"

The sudden quaver in Liz's voice seared Zoey's conscience. Although she had plenty of reasons, there was no indication that her grandmother was suspicious of her unexpected arrival.

Zoey sneaked a look at Matt and found those hazel eyes trained on her. Waiting for her response, too. "Mom told me that you'd just gotten out of the hospital."

"You talked to your mother?" There was no disguising the pleased surprise in Gran's voice.

"I thought maybe I could stay and help you out for awhile." Zoey didn't want to disappoint her grandmother by confessing that they hadn't really spoken—she'd listened to the voice mail message Sara Decker had left. "If you…need me, I mean," she added quickly.

The color drained from Liz's face again and Matt put a protective hand on her arm. "Liz? Are you all right?"

"I'm more than all right." Gran took a deep breath and patted his hand before turning a smile on Zoey that warmed her from the inside out. "I'd love for you to stay with me, sweetheart. And you are welcome for as long as you'd like."

Chapter Three

That was it?

No questions?

Because Matt had a truckload of them, even if Liz didn't.

Judging from the interaction he'd witnessed between the two women, it was clear they hadn't seen each other in quite a while. And it didn't take a trained counselor—which Matt happened to be—to figure out that some of Zoey's tension seemed to stem from her uncertainty over how she would be received.

But that didn't make sense, either. Liz was known for her hospitality. She was the kind of woman who encouraged people to drop in without an invitation.

"Matthew?" Liz turned to him. "Do you have time to help Zoey carry her things in?"

Before he could reply, Zoey surged to her feet. "That's okay, Gran, I don't need his help. I don't have much. Just some clothes."

And apparently she didn't want Liz to know those clothes were piled on the backseat of her vehicle.

A frown deepened the row of pleats across Liz's forehead. "Are you sure?"

"Yes. And I'm sure that…Pastor Wilde has other things to do instead of play bellhop."

To her nonexistent luggage, Matt thought.

Their eyes met. Hers begged him not to say the words out loud.

"I do have an appointment at nine." Matt took his cue and stood up. "I'm sure you two ladies have a lot of catching up to do."

"We do at that, don't we, Zoey?" Liz beamed. "I'll have a fresh pot of coffee on by the time you get settled."

"Gran, please." Zoey bit down on her lower lip. "I didn't come here so you could fuss over me. I came to fuss over you, remember?"

Liz closed her eyes, as if savoring something sweet. "I like the sound of that."

"Really?" Matt lifted a skeptical brow. "You might like the 'sound' of it and yet you fight it all the way."

"That's not completely true," Liz protested.

Matt looked at Zoey. "You did catch the word 'completely,' didn't you?"

Zoey's lips curved in a brief, tentative smile that had the power to derail his initial reservations like a runaway freight train.

"You can stay in your old bedroom, Zoey," Liz

went on. "I'm afraid, though, that it looks exactly the same way as it did when you left."

Your old bedroom?

Matt tried to hide his astonishment. The comment made it sound as if the arrangement had been permanent at one time.

Which made it even more unbelievable that Liz had never mentioned a granddaughter.

"I could stay in the carriage house," Zoey ventured. "That way, I won't be underfoot but I'll still be close by if you need me."

Liz waved her hand in the air, brushing away the comment the way she would a pesky fly. "What I *need* is a little noise in this drafty old house. There's plenty of room for the two of us."

"But…"

"And the carriage house isn't available," Liz interrupted.

"Oh." Zoey looked confused. "I thought maybe you and grandpa had gone ahead with your original plan to convert it into an apartment."

"Oh, we did," Liz said cheerfully. "That's why it isn't available. Matthew lives there now."

Zoey's gaze flew to his face. Matt expected to see dismay or even resentment in her eyes. All he saw was a resigned acceptance that had him struggling against a sudden urge to apologize.

He turned to Liz instead. "I'll come by later this afternoon," he promised. "And by the way, Kate said to remind you that tomorrow is pecan pie day, so she's going to stop over and drop off a piece."

"That's wonderful. Zoey and I will have to share." Liz lifted her face and Matt dutifully pressed a kiss against the weathered cheek.

"I'll be right back, Gran." Zoey started toward the door, then paused to level a stern look in her grandmother's direction. "Promise me that you won't lift a finger to do anything until I get back. *I'll* put a fresh pot of coffee on."

Liz sighed. "I promise."

Matt had sensed that Liz was beginning to tire but hadn't expected Zoey to notice. The fact that she had—and also that she knew her grandmother didn't like to sit still—put some of his concerns to rest.

Liz seemed genuinely thrilled that her granddaughter had shown up out of the blue.

Matt was happy for her, too, but that wasn't going to stop him from finding out just who Zoey Decker was.

And the real reason she'd come to Mirror Lake.

Up until the moment Gran had embraced her, Zoey had half-expected to be turned away, the way she had once pushed her grandparents away, declaring that she didn't need them.

But Gran had immediately put her fears to rest, with no hint of resentment or censure in her eyes.

Zoey had a long way to go to make amends, but at least Gran was willing to give her a chance.

"Here. This might help."

A cardboard box was deposited at her feet next to the Jeep. Zoey didn't have to turn around to know who was there. The breeze carried the faint scent of Matt's cologne, a clean, masculine scent that had, along with his smile, remained stubbornly lodged in her memory.

"Thank you." Zoey dropped an armful of jeans into the box, inwardly chiding herself for not taking the time to retrieve her suitcase from her landlord's storage unit.

A pink kneesock decorated with winged musical notes tumbled to the ground, but before Zoey could swoop down and retrieve it, Matt got there first.

"Here you go."

She plucked it from his hand.

Was there no end to the man's charity? Zoey wondered.

There will be. Just wait.

The thought almost made her drop the Bible she'd wrapped in a stack of T-shirts.

Matt propped a hip against the side of her car. In spite of his comment that he had to get back to the church for an appointment, he seemed in no hurry to leave. "Liz was happy to see you. I haven't seen her look so perky in quite a while. A lot of us have been concerned about her. Contracting pneumonia was bad enough, but the complications that kept her in the hospital an extra week took quite a toll on her health."

"I didn't find out that she was in the hospital until yesterday," Zoey muttered.

That was her fault, too.

Her parents had grown accustomed to her avoiding contact with them. They never failed to send a card for her birthday or on holidays, but the majority of communication had been reduced to a few stilted conversations spread out over the year.

Regret sliced through Zoey. She could have been here sooner. Could have sat next to Gran's hospital bed, the way Gran had once sat next to hers…

The memories pressed down on her conscience and she tried to shake them away. The effort drained Zoey's already-depleted reserve of energy. She picked up a tasseled silk pillow, resisting the urge to bury her face in it.

"How far did you drive?"

Here it was. Question Number One. Zoey braced herself for the inquisition.

"A few hours. I live near Lake Delton."

"Wisconsin Dells area?"

Zoey nodded curtly, wishing he would go away. She swept up the box as he bent down to retrieve it. "I've got it."

Matt straightened, parking his hands on his hips. Zoey tried not to stare. He'd been attractive in loose-fitting sweats. In faded jeans, a marled blue fisherman's sweater and hiking boots, he looked more like the cover model for a popular outdoor men's magazine.

"Liz is special," Matt said after a moment. "Everyone loves her. She sort of became my adoptive grandmother when I moved to town…" He paused.

Here it comes, Zoey thought.

The Warning.

You better not take advantage of her a) hospitality, b) generosity, c) kindness. Or d) all of the above.

"I'm glad you're here, Zoey. She needs her family."

Family.

The word echoed through the hollow places in Zoey's heart.

It was the best…and the worst…thing he could have said.

What had he said?

Matt watched myriad emotions skim through Zoey's expressive eyes, as if he'd skipped a rock across the lake and created ripples across the surface.

"It looks like she has you, too." Zoey looked down at the ground. The winter sunlight had gained strength as the morning wore on and brought out a cherry-cola sheen in the tangle of dark curls that skimmed her shoulders.

"She does." Matt wondered why Zoey had such a difficult time looking at him. "She has a lot of people who care about her."

Zoey slammed the door of the Jeep, triggering an avalanche of rust that rained onto his boots.

Matt thought he heard her groan.

"Are you sure you don't need help with that?"

"I can manage on my own."

Without even trying, he'd managed to insult her again.

"But…thank you." Zoey's voice was so soft, Matt had to strain to hear the words. "I'm glad you've been here. To look out for Gran." Her expression turned wistful as she stared at the house.

She continued to surprise him. An intriguing mix of toughness and vulnerability. Honesty and secrets.

"I'm sorry about the carriage house," he heard himself say. "After the last pastor retired, the congregation voted to sell the parsonage to cut down on costs. Liz mentioned she had a separate apartment and asked if I'd be interested in living there."

Matt remembered the conversation as if it had taken place the day before. Liz had not only offered him a place to live, but she'd also informed him that she and Jonathan had always planned to use the extra apartment space as a "blessing" to others and refused to accept any rent.

"Don't worry about it." Zoey's slim shoulders lifted in a shrug. "Gran's right. There's plenty of room in the house and I'll be able to hear her if she gets up in the night."

"I'll sleep better knowing you're there, that's for sure."

"Will you?" she asked evenly.

For a man who'd frequently been told that he was

"eloquent," Matt didn't know what to say. It was almost as if she expected him to be suspicious of her.

"Yes." Based on what he'd seen so far, it was the truth.

Zoey took a step back. "I better go inside before Gran decides to put fresh sheets on the bed."

"It was nice to meet you. Again." Matt smiled in a blatant attempt to coax one out of her. Because smiles were supposed to be contagious, weren't they?

It didn't work.

She pivoted away from him, hugging the box against her chest.

Matt had the distinct impression that Zoey Decker kept her secrets just as close.

Zoey collapsed facedown on the comforter covering the canopy bed and immediately sank into a cloud of lavender-scented chiffon. Lace from the pillow sham ticked her nose so she rolled over and stared at the ceiling. Above her head, an uneven constellation of plastic, glow-in-the-dark stars circled the antique light fixture.

Oh, Gran.

Zoey wasn't sure whether to laugh or cry. Although she'd been warned that her old bedroom hadn't undergone any significant changes, Zoey hadn't been prepared to open the door and be instantly transported into the past, courtesy of a frothy pink and white time machine.

Everything remained exactly the way she remembered it.

Exactly the way she'd left it.

Her gaze traveled over the interior of the room, pausing to linger on the distressed ivory writing desk and matching bookcase. The latter still sported the row of first-edition Nancy Drew mysteries that Gran had proudly offered for her entertainment. An oversized tufted ottoman, complete with gold buttons and a tasseled skirt, remained in front of the window as if it had been nailed in place, its strategic position designed to encourage what her Grandpa Jonathan had often referred to as "pondering."

At sixteen, Zoey had put that particular piece of furniture to good use. She had sat cross-legged on it for hours, staring out the window.

Pondering her escape.

Time—both in the push and shove of the real world and, more recently, on her knees—had slowly begun to alter her perspective.

Her grandparents hadn't been overly strict, but Zoey had been looking for a fight. Any rules, no matter how reasonable, were turned into a battle ground. She hadn't wanted to give her grandparents a difficult time. No, what she'd wanted was to get her *parents'* attention.

Zoey remembered how many times her grandparents had tried to get close to her, but she'd always pushed them away. After she moved out, that pattern had continued, like the steps of an intricate dance. Zoey had practiced—and perfected—it over the years.

Until she realized that God hadn't left her side.

He had been there to take her hand and lift her up, but Zoey had never expected He would lead her back to Mirror Lake.

"It won't be so bad," she told the stuffed bear perched on the windowsill. "Gran's practically a shut-in. I'll stick close to the house until she's back on her feet. People will hardly know I'm here."

Zoey sat up, debating whether she should check on Gran again. It was difficult to acknowledge how much of her grandmother's energy had been stolen by the bout of pneumonia and an extended stay in the hospital. Gran had always seemed so…ageless. But Zoey had come face to face with reality when she returned to the house and found Gran dozing on the sofa.

With her eyes closed, Liz looked so small and frail that Zoey wanted to wrap her arms around the thin shoulders and share some of her own strength.

She'd draped an afghan over Gran's lap instead, intending to beat a quiet retreat and finish unpacking the rest of her things.

"Zoey?" Gran had stirred before she reached the door. "Are you still here?"

"You aren't going to get rid of me that easily."

Gran looked troubled. "I wouldn't want to."

Zoey hoped they would eventually get to the place

where the past didn't cast a shadow on every conversation. Every innocent comment.

"Gran, why don't you finish your nap while I unpack?"

"That sounded more like an order than a suggestion." Gran had chuckled, the sparkle back in her eyes. "Between you and Matthew, I'm going to be spoiled rotten."

You and Matthew.

Her grandmother's words cycled through Zoey's mind and she yanked the pillow over her head. It didn't, however, blot out the image of Matt Wilde's handsome face or erase the warmth of his smile from her memory.

Maybe, Zoey thought, it was all right to hold onto the memory of that smile a little bit longer.

When people started talking about her—and Zoey knew they would—she was pretty sure she wouldn't see it again.

Chapter Four

"Gran! What are you doing?" Zoey crossed her arms over her chest and tried to stare her grandmother down.

The house had been so quiet while she'd finished putting away her things that Zoey assumed Gran was still sleeping. Not standing on her tiptoes in front of the fireplace, attacking the flock of porcelain birds perched on the mantle with a bright-yellow feather duster.

"Dusting?" Gran stared right back.

"I can see that." Zoey's lips twitched. At least her grandmother had the grace to look guilty. "My next question is, *why* are you dusting?"

"Because I could have sworn I heard one of these poor birds sneeze."

Zoey gave up trying to keep a straight face and laughed. "I have a great idea. It involves you sitting in your favorite chair, sipping a cup of tea by the fire, while I take care of the birds. And anything else that you're planning to clean the minute my back is turned."

"A cup of tea sounds wonderful, but sharing your company while I drink it sounds even better."

There was no mistaking the sincerity in her grandmother's voice.

Regret tangled with gratitude. For the past six years, Zoey had told herself that the best thing she could do for her grandparents was stay away from Mirror Lake. She'd caused enough heartache without an occasional visit stirring up the past.

Zoey was beginning to realize she'd been wrong to let that particular rationalization create such a rift between them. But she hadn't known how to bridge it, not until her mother had left the message expressing her concern about Gran managing on her own while she recovered from pneumonia.

Zoey had been praying that God would help her move forward, but she hadn't expected it would mean facing the past. It was as if He had opened a door for reconciliation and left it up to Zoey to decide whether to walk through it. A few hours later, she'd been driving north.

"I'll make the—" Gran paused when Zoey raised an eyebrow.

"I'll let you make the tea."

"Great. Then we have a deal." Zoey patted the arm of the chair and waited for her grandmother to comply. Gran looked more rested from her nap, but the purple smudges under her eyes hadn't faded. The steps she took were slow and careful, as if she had to concentrate on every one.

Zoey resisted the urge to hover as Liz lowered herself into the chair.

"I'm afraid that I'm used to being useful," she admitted.

"I know." Zoey draped an afghan over her grandmother's lap. Ten years was a long time but not long enough for her to forget how Gran loved to keep busy, deliberately placing herself at the center of a whirlwind of activity, especially when it came to her church.

Unbidden, Matt Wilde's face appeared in her mind. She still couldn't believe the church had hired someone so young.

And single.

Zoey ignored the mischievous inner voice. So she'd happened to notice that the pastor hadn't been wearing a wedding ring. What difference did it make? A man as kind and drop-dead gorgeous as Matt had to be in a serious relationship. Probably even engaged...

And why on earth do you care?

Even if she had time to date, which she didn't, Zoey knew she would never consider a serious relationship with someone involved in ministry. As the daughter of a pastor-turned-missionary, Zoey had buckled under the weight of peoples' expectations. There was no way she would put herself into that situation again.

Not that someone like Matthew Wilde would ever ask her to...

Zoey put the brakes on those wayward thoughts before they could take her any further down that dangerous path.

"You'll be back on your feet in no time, Gran," she promised. "And you *are* being useful. You're going to tell me what to do, remember?"

"All right." Gran smiled. "While you finish dusting, you have to tell me everything that's happened to you in the last ten years."

Zoey took a deep breath. "I'd rather tell you about the last six months."

A look of understanding dawned and tears sprang into Liz's eyes. "You're a believer now, aren't you?"

"I've been a believer a long time," Zoey said softly. "Now, I would have to say that I'm a...follower."

"Delia Peake is here to see you, Pastor." Cheryl Mullins, the part-time church secretary, looked up as Matt walked in. "She wanted to wait in your office."

"And you didn't want to tell her no." Matt grinned.

"I'd rather sharpen a pencil with my teeth."

"Ouch."

"Exactly." Cheryl patted her very pregnant belly. "I'm a month from my due date and the doctor told me to avoid stress."

"Then you made the right decision." Matt glanced at the clock on the wall. He usually left the church at four, but experience had taught him that pastors didn't hold to regular hours. He was on call 24/7.

And he wouldn't want it any other way.

"You don't have to stick around, Cheryl. I can lock up when I leave."

His secretary didn't bother to hide her relief. "Great.

I'll see you tomorrow."

As Matt walked down the narrow hallway, he heard the muffled *tap tap tap* of Delia's walking cane against the faded Berber carpet in his office.

"Hello, Mrs. Peake."

She had bypassed a comfortable chair by the window and commandeered the one behind the desk. His desk.

Matt's lips twitched as he pulled up another chair.

"Pastor Wilde." From the first time they'd met, Delia insisted on addressing him more formally than the rest of his congregation, most of whom called him by his first name. "How is Liz?"

It had become a common question over the past few weeks, given the fact that Matt was not only Liz's pastor, but also her closest neighbor. "She seems to be doing a little better."

Especially now.

For most of the day, Matt had found his thoughts drifting back to Zoey. Wondering how she and Liz were doing. What they were talking about. When one of the men in his congregation had called and asked for some insight on a passage of scripture, Matt had jumped at the chance to focus his attention on something else. And it didn't hurt that their discussion had taken place while they split a cord of firewood.

After Matt was hired, he made sure people knew he wanted to see them for more than an hour on Sunday mornings. He wanted the majority of his ministry to take place outside the walls of the church.

Delia pursed her lips. "When I called her yesterday, Liz wasn't in a very talkative mood."

"I'm sure she was just tired." Matt linked his hands behind his head. "What can I do for you, Mrs. Peake?"

The question didn't bring about the results he'd hoped for—nudging Delia back on track.

"She's a stubborn woman, our Liz. When I visited her at the hospital last week, she mentioned that she's still planning to direct the Easter cantata next month." Delia shook her head. "Of course I told her that she wouldn't be in any shape to take on that responsibility this year."

"Of course you did." Matt tried not to wince. He had deliberately avoided bringing up the subject of the cantata to Liz, knowing that she didn't need anything else to worry about.

"Well, someone has to make her listen to reason." Delia agreed, happy to have accepted the role. "There isn't a lot of time to pull it together. Some people think we should simply cancel it this year."

Judging from her tone, it was clear she was one of them.

"Let's see what the Lord has to say before we make a decision," Matt suggested mildly. "Someone else might step forward and volunteer to take Liz's place this year."

Delia harrumphed. "I suppose that could happen."

"I'll talk to Liz when the time is *right*." Matt pressed down on the last word, hoping to get his point across. "We have at least a week before a final decision needs to be made. By that time, Liz should have a better idea whether or not she feels up to directing the cantata."

At the moment, Matt couldn't think of anyone more capable of organizing the special service that Church of the Pines held every Easter, but it was a lot of work and he didn't want to jeopardize Liz's recovery. Still, Matt knew her well enough to know that if she were pushed to make a decision, she would say "yes" simply to relieve him of the burden of having to find someone else.

"You can count on me keeping a close eye on her." Delia's pink-tipped walking cane struck the floor, punctuating the statement like an exclamation point. "I'm planning to stop by her place for a visit every day until she can get out and about."

For some reason, the thought of Delia and Zoey coming face to face unsettled him. The older woman had good intentions, but not many people saw them, hidden as they were behind a rather formidable personality. The wave of protectiveness that crashed over Matt surprised him. Especially given the fact that Zoey had let him know, in no uncertain terms, that she could take care of herself.

He hesitated. "I'm sure Liz would appreciate the thought, but I don't think that will be necessary."

"What do you mean?"

The sudden gleam of interest in the woman's eyes made Matt regret bringing it up.

"She has family staying with her now."

"Family." Delia brightened. "Paul and Sara came back from Africa for a visit? I'm sure Liz is thrilled. They haven't been back since Jonathan's funeral."

"It's not her son. Her granddaughter, Zoey, is going to stay with Liz for awhile."

Delia's eyes bulged. "Zoey Decker is *here?* In Mirror Lake? Staying with Liz?"

"Yes, to all three questions." Matt tipped his head, puzzled by the strange reaction. "Do you…know Zoey?"

Delia's expression turned as bleak as a January morning.

"Unfortunately, everyone in Mirror Lake knows Zoey Decker."

"Will you set the table for three, please, sweetheart?"

The simple endearment warmed Zoey's heart, especially when it came on the heels of a lengthy conversation in which she'd condensed the ups and downs of the last ten years. And there'd definitely been more downs than ups.

The tea in their cups had cooled while she talked and Gran had listened. Zoey thought that telling her story would have once again left her feeling burdened by the past. Instead, she felt curiously relieved. Lighthearted.

Gran had forgiven her for the mistakes she'd made—and the ones she'd compounded by separating herself from her family. Zoey could see it in her eyes. It occurred to her that it had been there all along. From the moment she'd arrived.

And maybe, although Zoey could barely wrap her mind around it, even before.

If only she were finding it as easy to forgive herself.

She pulled a wooden chair out from the table, a gentle reminder to Gran that she was in charge of kitchen duty.

"You're having company for supper tonight?" Zoey asked as she zeroed in on one of the kitchen cabinets and opened the door. A set of powder-blue stoneware dishes was stacked neatly on the other side, the way she remembered. Strange how she now found comfort in the things she'd spent years trying to forget.

"*We're* having company," her grandmother corrected. "Matthew has a standing invitation every Thursday night."

Zoey stifled a groan. By now Matt—*the pastor*— would know everything about her. And she doubted he would be as forgiving as her grandmother. "I don't want to intrude on your time together. I can eat upstairs. Or in the family room."

Anywhere but at the kitchen table.

Liz brushed aside the suggestion. "You won't be intruding, Zoey. I'm sure Matt is anxious to get to know you."

Probably to make sure I'm not stealing your silver spoon collection, Zoey wanted to say.

To hide her dismay, she lifted the lid on the Noah's ark cookie jar that still occupied the corner next to the sink. Sure enough, it was filled with molasses cookies, the crisp tops sparkling with sugar. Gran had shared them with the people who stopped in for a visit as generously as she gave of her time. And prayers.

Sometimes Zoey wondered if Gran's faithful prayers had been instrumental in leading her back to faith.

"I couldn't keep that cookie jar full when you lived here. Help yourself."

Hearing the amusement in Gran's voice, Zoey blinked back the unexpected tears that stung her eyes. The time she'd lived in Mirror Lake had been so short, she hadn't realized how many memories remained cradled in her heart.

She tried to match her grandmother's tone. "Aren't you afraid it will spoil my appetite if I eat dessert first?"

"Then we'll call the cookies an appetizer." Gran

winked and held out her hand. "I won't tell if you don't."

Zoey dipped into the ceramic jar and pulled out two cookies, one for Gran and one for herself. "Do you want me to heat up one of the casseroles for supper?"

"Oh, no. Thursday is pizza night. Matthew started it a few months ago."

Matthew again.

She forced a smile. "I don't mind making dinner but I think that you and Pastor Wilde…well, you know what they say, Gran. Three's a crowd, right?"

"I always liked 'the more, the merrier' myself."

Zoey froze at the sound of a voice behind her. The voice belonging to the man who'd already managed to sneak up on her twice in one day. She was afraid to look at him. Afraid to see censure or—even worse— disapproval in the hazel eyes that had been full of concern earlier that morning.

"You're right on time, Matthew," Gran sang out. "Yesterday I have to admit that I was feeling a little sorry for myself and tonight I'm having supper with my two favorite people."

Zoey dared a glance in Matt's direction. He wasn't glaring at her in disapproval. He wasn't glaring at all.

"I didn't stop by for supper," Matt said, a smile playing at the corners of his lips. "You just got home from the hospital yesterday and you have your granddaughter visiting. That means I'm officially releasing you from the burden of my company tonight."

Zoey was immune to his smile. She really was. And it wasn't as if it were directed at her.

"Don't be ridiculous, Matthew," Gran clucked her tongue. "Your company isn't a burden. Is it, Zoey?"

Zoey hesitated a split second too long. "No, not at all."

Matt sauntered in, altogether too attractive for Zoey's peace of mind. He peeled off a fleece-lined leather jacket that emphasized the width of his shoulders and draped it over the back of the chair. "In that case, I'd love to stay."

"Wonderful." Gran clapped her hands together.

Wonderful.

Zoey's knees went a little weak at the thought of spending more time in Matt's company.

She made a silent calculation in an attempt to steady them. And her nerves. It only took twelve minutes to bake a frozen pizza. With luck, the pastor would be gone in an hour. Maybe less.

Zoey scooted over to the freezer, wishing she could crawl inside, and scanned the contents. Towers of plastic containers, neatly labeled, crowded the small space.

"Where's the pizza, Gran?"

Her grandmother chuckled. "You have to make it."

"I know." Zoey glanced over her shoulder and her gaze snagged with Matt's. The slow smile he aimed in her direction shot through her like a comet. She tore her gaze away and focused on Gran. Much safer. "But I don't *see* one to make."

"I'm sorry." Gran looked anything but. In fact, she looked as if she were enjoying Zoey's confusion. "Matthew and I make the pizza from scratch."

"From…scratch?"

"That's right." Matt answered the question. "But don't worry. Liz and I will walk you through it. It isn't difficult."

Liz lifted her hand and covered a delicate yawn. "Actually, I'm feeling a little tired so I think I'll sit this one out," she said. "Let me know when it's ready."

"Gran!" Zoey choked on the word.

"Don't worry. Matthew knows his way around the kitchen." Gran toddled off without a backward glance.

That's not what Zoey was worried about.

"I guess it's just the two of us," Matt said.

Zoey managed a smile.

"I guess it is."

Chapter Five

Zoey didn't look happy at the way things had turned out. Matt, however, didn't mind a bit. Even though he had been willing to bow out of his standing Thursday night dinner invitation with Liz, he had secretly hoped she would invite him to stay.

On his way over from the church, Matt had had a lengthy conversation with God about Zoey.

Who, he suddenly noticed, hadn't moved since Liz left the room.

What could he say to put her at ease?

"You changed clothes."

Zoey's eyes widened.

Okay, that wasn't it. But he couldn't help but notice that the oversized sweater had been replaced by a long-sleeved T-shirt that outlined the subtle curves of her slender frame. Apple-green ballet shoes peeked out below the hem of a multicolored, ankle-length skirt.

"Yes." Color bloomed in Zoey's cheeks. "What I was wearing this morning…that was my costume."

"Costume?" To hide his surprise, Matt opened the refrigerator and pulled out a package of crisp green peppers and fresh mushrooms. Staples in Liz's kitchen for what had become a Thursday night tradition.

"I left right after work last night. When my mother called and left the message about Gran, I wanted to get to Mirror Lake as soon as possible."

The sincerity in Zoey's voice was unmistakable, but Matt couldn't help but wonder why it had been so long since she'd visited.

He wanted to know more about her, but he wanted it to come straight from Zoey, not someone else. Delia Peake had seemed more than willing to explain her negative reaction to the news of Zoey's return had Matt given her the opportunity. But he would never encourage a member of his congregation, or anyone else for that matter, to spread gossip, no matter what the situation. So he'd declined to hear it.

"A costume." Matt tilted his head. "What do you do?"

"I work at a dinner theater in the Wisconsin Dells."

"That sounds like fun. In what capacity?"

Zoey's lips parted but no sound came out. The sudden confusion in her eyes made Matt wonder if she'd had to defend her chosen career in the past.

"I'm part of the cast," Zoey said after a moment. "We rotate shows throughout the year and offer special performances over the holidays. Everything we do is family-friendly."

"I've heard that part of the state is a great vacation spot but I've never been there." Matt leaned over, snagged a mushroom out of the bowl and popped it into his mouth.

Zoey nodded but appeared to relax a little. "I took a short leave of absence to come back and help Gran."

"How long do you plan on staying?" Matt couldn't explain how, in the space of a few hours, he'd gone from questioning Zoey moving in with Liz to feeling disappointed that it was only temporary.

"I wasn't sure how long Gran would need me, so I asked for two weeks off. My understudy was thrilled, of course. She complains that she's never going to be discovered by a Hollywood talent agent if I refuse to get sick or take a personal day once in a while."

Matt processed that information as he dumped the flour and yeast into a mixing bowl. Liz had taught him how to make the crust from scratch, and now he'd done it so often he didn't need to look at a recipe anymore.

"Which play are you doing now?" He sat down across from her at the table, deliberately turning his attention to the task in front of him.

"We'll be performing a musical called *Once Upon a Castle*. Kind of a modern Cinderella story," Zoey explained. "Most of the performances are popular Broadway plays, but sometimes my director will use an original script when we want to put on a show with audience participation."

"So which part do you play?" Given the fact that Zoey had mentioned an understudy, Matt had a hunch she had a major role.

"Ella Cinders."

Matt laughed.

"Hey, don't make fun! The children love it." Zoey slapped the back of his hand when he reached for a slice of pepper.

The playful, completely unexpected, touch squeezed the air out of Matt's lungs.

Their eyes met, and Zoey lurched to her feet.

"I'll be right back," she muttered. "I better go check on Gran."

What on earth had she been thinking?

She hadn't, that was the trouble.

Because if she would have been thinking, Zoey would have remembered that Matt was her grand-mother's neighbor. Her *pastor*.

She hadn't expected to be on the receiving end of that heart-stopping smile again, let alone to be treated as if she were a person he was genuinely interested in getting to know rather than the town pariah.

Was it possible he hadn't asked someone about her yet?

If that were the case, Zoey wasn't quite sure what to do. It was only a matter of time before Matt found out the truth. Maybe she should simply tell him and get it over with…but the thought of seeing the warmth in those hazel eyes glaze over with disapproval caused the knot in her stomach to tighten.

Matt Wilde was a complication Zoey hadn't expected to find when she'd returned to Mirror Lake. An all too *attractive* complication.

"Is the pizza done already?" Gran looked up from her knitting as Zoey burst into the parlor.

"Ah, not yet." She felt the color rise in her cheeks. "I wanted to see if you needed anything." And she'd needed to escape.

"Not a thing." Gran looked perfectly content as the bright aquamarine knitting needles clicked together in her lap. "I'm so glad you and Matthew are getting acquainted. With your parents living in Africa and me all alone now, he's been more like family…" She broke off with a look of dismay. "I didn't mean that the way it sounded, sweetheart."

Zoey forced a smile. "I know you didn't, Gran."

Concern cast a shadow over Liz's face. "I can be so thoughtless at times," she murmured.

Zoey dropped to her knees by her grandmother's chair. "You aren't thoughtless at all. And I'm glad you have good friends who stop by to check on you. Have dinner with you. It must be lonely without Grandpa."

"It is." Gran's eyes misted, as if the grief was still fresh.

As different as night and day, her grandparents had been one of those rare couples whose love had only grown stronger over time. Zoey remembered rolling her eyes when her grandpa would tease her grandmother until she dissolved into giggles like a school girl. The way they would reach for each other's hands while walking down the street…or at the dinner table in prayer.

"I wish…" Zoey's voice cracked under the weight of her regrets.

Liz squeezed her hand, as if she understood. "I appreciate your checking on me, but you better help Matt. He tends to make a mess if I'm not there to stop him."

"I heard that!" A cheerful masculine voice called out.

Zoey winced, wondering what else he'd heard. She had forgotten how thin the walls were between the rooms.

"All right," she agreed. "But if you need anything, let me know." *Soon.*

As soon as Zoey walked into the kitchen, she realized her plan had backfired. Matt had finished his assigned task and, with chef's knife in hand, was armed and ready to help her.

She slid into the chair across the table from him and held her breath, waiting for him to pick up where the conversation had left off. Instead, Matt continued chopping up peppers. When she didn't move, he raised an eyebrow.

"Can't get your knife to work?"

Zoey almost smiled.

"I know they can be kind of tricky."

Now she did smile.

"I'll figure it out." Zoey grabbed another pepper out of the bowl and set to work.

The silence should have been uncomfortable, but Matt seemed perfectly at ease. They worked together in a companionable silence. By the time the pizza was ready, instead of watching the clock tick off the minutes, Zoey couldn't believe the time had passed so quickly.

The timer went off and Zoey jumped up. "I'll take it out."

She opened a drawer next to the oven and found it filled with measuring cups and baking utensils.

"The drawer on the left."

"Gran was right. You do know your way around the kitchen." To cover up her mistake—and the guilt that came from knowing how long she'd been away—Zoey tried to inject a teasing note in her voice. And failed miserably.

Matt looked down at her, a frown settling between his brows. Zoey braced herself, waiting for the attack. The "if-you'd-come-around-more-often-you'd-know-where-the-potholders-were-too" reminder.

"The pizza looks great. I'll get Liz" was all Matt said.

He left the kitchen and Zoey finished getting the table ready. She put out a bowl of fresh spinach with chopped tomatoes and a gelatin salad, one of several lined up like colorful jewels on the shelf in the refrigerator. Her grandmother's friends had dropped off enough food to feed a small army.

On impulse, Zoey lit the pillar candle in the center of the table. It cast a warm glow in the room.

"Everything looks lovely." Gran swept in on Matt's arm, not looking nearly as tired as she'd claimed to be when she left them alone on kitchen duty.

Zoey's heart started beating in double-time as a thought suddenly occurred to her.

No, Gran wouldn't dare...not a woman who believed it was God who brought a couple together, without any help from earthly matchmakers. Or well-meaning grandmothers.

"What would you like to drink, Liz?" Matt pulled a chair away from the table.

"Water, please."

"I'll get it." Zoey was pretty sure she remembered where Gran kept that.

As she opened the refrigerator door and reached for the pitcher, she heard the front door open.

"Hellooo! Is anyone home?"

Matt's head jerked up. Something in the look that he and her grandmother exchanged sent off warning bells inside of Zoey's head. She heard a staccato *tap tap tapping* noise against the hardwood floor. Ten seconds later a woman appeared in the doorway.

Zoey hadn't recognized the voice but she remembered the face.

Delia Peake.

"Liz, I thought you'd be finished eating supper by

now." Somehow Delia made the statement sound like an accusation. She leaned on her cane, her sharp gaze sweeping over the three place settings grouped around the steaming pizza. "This is certainly a cozy scene. Hello, Pastor Wilde."

"Mrs. Peake." Matt rose to his feet with a smile. "I didn't expect to see you again so soon."

The circles of rouge on Delia's cheeks deepened in color and expanded. "I brought over the new pattern that Esther picked out for our next knitting project."

"You didn't have to go to all that trouble, Delia," Liz protested.

"It was no trouble at all." Delia might have been speaking to Gran, but she was looking straight at Zoey. As if she couldn't believe she was really there.

"You remember my granddaughter, Zoey," Gran said.

"Hello." The frosty look on Delia's face said that yes, she remembered her.

"Mrs. Peake."

They both remembered.

Delia had been opposed to Zoey moving in with her grandparents right from the start, arguing that a teenage granddaughter, and a rebellious one at that, would only turn their lives upside down. It hadn't helped that all her fears had come to pass, and then some.

She knew that people like Delia Peake would regard her with suspicion. People believed what they wanted to believe. Zoey had discovered that following the accident. It had been easier to lay blame on the Decker's troubled granddaughter, an "outsider," rather than on Tyler Curtis, the charming, popular teenage quarterback who'd grown up in Mirror Lake.

Even now, the memory continued to cast a shadow over Zoey's life. Her physical injuries from the accident had healed within weeks. The bruises on her soul were taking longer.

Zoey had resented Delia's interference at the time, but now she understood the woman's concern stemmed from her long-standing friendship with Gran.

It was natural to want to protect the people you cared about.

She knew it wouldn't be easy seeing her grandmother's friends again, but facing Delia was even more difficult than Zoey had imagined.

One step forward, right, Lord?

She took a deep breath, set the water pitcher down on the table and summoned a smile. "Would you like to join us for dinner, Mrs. Peake? We have plenty."

Out of the corner of her eye, Zoey saw that Matt looked as taken aback by the invitation as her grandmother.

"Join you? *Well*." Delia leaned on the word. "I'm afraid I can't. My son will be stopping over tonight to fix a leaky faucet in the bathroom. But…thank you." She cleared her throat. "And Liz, let me know if you need any help with the new pattern. You should have plenty of time to work on it because Esther is going to postpone our next meeting until you're feeling better."

"That's very sweet, but I don't expect everyone to tailor their schedule to mine," Liz said.

"We don't mind waiting. It wouldn't be the same without you anyway." Delia's expression softened.

"You could meet here."

Three pairs of eyes turned in her direction.

Oh, no. She'd actually said it out loud.

Nice going, Zoey. So much for your plan to avoid people.

But that didn't mean she wanted Gran to be cut off from her friends and some of the activities she enjoyed.

She could always…hide.

"Here?" A thoughtful look came into her grandmother's eyes.

"Why not?" Zoey said faintly, although she could come up with a hundred reasons. None of which had come to mind, of course, when she'd made the impulsive suggestion.

"Delia?" Liz's gaze shifted to her friend.

"I suppose that would work. I could make the phone calls." Delia appeared to warm to the idea as Zoey's feet got colder.

"I *would* love to see everyone," Gran said. "All right, Delia. Tomorrow night. Seven o'clock. In my parlor."

Tomorrow night?

Zoey swallowed hard.

She'd hoped for a little more time to get used to the idea.

"I suppose I should let you get back to your dinner." Delia's sigh made it clear she would much rather join them.

"I'll walk you out, Mrs. Peake." Matt linked his arm through Delia's and escorted her out of the kitchen. When he returned a few minutes later and took his seat at the table, Zoey couldn't help but notice that he looked a little grim.

Zoey bit her lip. Maybe Delia had taken the opportunity to explain the reason behind her less-than-warm welcome.

"Matthew, would you like to pray?" Liz asked.

"Of course."

Zoey bowed her head but jumped when she felt Gran take hold of one of her hands...and Matt the other. The warm press of his fingers sent little electrical charges shooting up her arm. It was all she could do not to yank her hand away.

"God, thank You so much for today. For this food and Your many blessings. Thank You that Liz is out of the hospital, and we ask for Your continued healing now that she is home. Thank You for Zoey and her willingness to put her life on hold in order to be here, where she's needed."

Zoey opened her eyes but Matt's prayer continued to echo through her soul.

In her self-imposed exile, she hadn't felt needed in a long time.

Chapter Six

"You're still here."

Matt heard Zoey's steps falter as she walked into the kitchen and spotted him at the sink, finishing up the dishes. Her look of dismay told him that she'd thought—or more likely *hoped*—he'd already left.

"I thought I'd straighten up while you helped Liz get settled for the night," he explained.

"I can take over now. I'm sure you're anxious to get home." Zoey straightened her shoulders, as if preparing for battle. But what—or who—was she fighting against? That's what Matt couldn't figure out.

"I don't mind. It's not like I have a long drive home, you know." He flashed an easy smile. "I live next door."

Zoey didn't respond to the gentle teasing. If anything, it looked as though she was tempted to bolt. Again.

Matt tried to trace the change in her mood to its source.

They had worked well enough together while preparing the pizza.

Some of the tension had eased from Zoey's slim shoulders while they chopped up vegetables. But after Delia had left and Matt had given thanks for the meal, it was as if a wall had gone up between them.

Matt hadn't attempted to draw her out during dinner, afraid that if he did, she would find a reason to excuse herself from the table. She seemed content to listen while he caught Liz up on some of the things happening at church during her stay at the hospital. For a woman who made her living performing on a stage, Zoey Decker certainly shied away from being the center of attention.

The truth was, Matt could have finished the dishes and been long gone already. But he'd lingered in the kitchen, hoping to have another opportunity to talk to Zoey.

He wasn't sure why he felt so drawn to her. Especially when she seemed so uncomfortable around *him*.

That was another thing Matt couldn't figure out. Sure, there were always a few people who fidgeted and stammered when they discovered a pastor in their midst, but for the most part he was able to put them at ease. To draw them out. One of his professors at the seminary had gone so far as to call it a gift.

Dr. Woods probably would've lowered Matt's grade if he witnessed Zoey's reaction to him.

He turned back to the sink and waited. A few

seconds later, Zoey joined him there but maintained a careful distance. Not that it mattered. Even with a foot of space between them, every nerve ending in Matt's body kicked into high alert.

Zoey picked up a towel and reached for one of the china plates in the dish drainer. "I think Gran must be the only person in Mirror Lake who doesn't have a dishwasher."

"She probably is." Matt gave the soapy cloth in his hand a meaningful wave. "She claims that washing dishes by hand gives a person time to think."

"She used to tell me the same thing when I was sixteen. I didn't believe her then either."

Sixteen.

Another piece of the puzzle that was Zoey. Matt realized that getting to know her was going to take time. And patience.

Somehow, he knew it would be worth the effort.

"Does Gran still hang the sheets outside on the line to dry?"

"Every Monday morning, April through October." Matt's heart contracted at the pensive look on Zoey's face.

"I always wondered where Gran got all her energy," she said. "Grandpa used to say that just watching her made him want to take a nap."

"I know, she amazes me," Matt agreed. "You are going to have quite a challenge convincing her to rest, you know."

"I already figured that out." Zoey's lips curved into

a smile. "She said that she needs something to do, so I told her that giving me orders definitely falls into that category."

Matt laughed. "You are a wise woman, Zoey Decker."

The smile faded.

"You don't agree?" Seeing the shadow that skimmed across Zoey's expressive face, Matt pushed a little, wondering where the question would take him.

She put the last plate back in the cupboard. "I think we're done here."

Matt inwardly winced.

Right into a brick wall, that's where it had taken him.

"You're working too hard."

Oops.

Zoey glanced over her shoulder and saw her grandmother standing a few feet away, arms folded over her chest.

The last time Zoey had checked, Liz had fallen asleep on the sofa while watching one of her favorite afternoon programs. Zoey had hoped to finish mopping the floor in the front hallway before she woke up.

"I like to keep busy." It was the truth. And it kept her thoughts from straying to her grandmother's next-door neighbor.

Most of the time, anyway.

To her relief, Matt had left right after they'd finishing cleaning up the kitchen the night before. Unfortunately, his absence hadn't prevented his smile from continuing to linger in her thoughts.

Throughout the night and right into the next day.

"What are your plans for the rest of the afternoon?" Gran's voice tugged Zoey back to the present.

"I thought I would put in a few loads of laundry and start supper. Straighten up the parlor before your friends arrive." Zoey saw the tiny frown that appeared on Liz's brow. "Unless you have something else you'd rather have me do?"

"I want you to take a walk," Liz said. "You've been cooped up in the house with me all day."

"I like being cooped up with you." And taking a walk definitely increased the possibility of running into people Zoey remembered from the past.

People who remembered *her.*

Zoey wasn't ready for that. Not yet.

"That's very sweet, Zoey, but I do admit to having an ulterior motive."

Zoey grinned. "I don't believe it."

"It's true." Her grandmother's eyes twinkled. "I was hoping you wouldn't mind running a quick errand for me while you were out."

Zoey sucked in a breath. Released it slowly. This was the reason she had come back to Mirror Lake, she reminded herself. To help Gran out. "Of course not. What do you need?"

"I looked at the pattern Delia dropped off last night

and I'll need two more skeins of yarn for our next knitting project. I wouldn't be in such a rush if the group wasn't meeting here tonight."

See what you got yourself into, Zoey? And you have no one to blame but yourself!

"Some of the girls order their yarn off the Internet now, but I always buy mine at the variety store," Liz was saying. "It carries a good selection and I like to support the local businesses."

The variety store. On Main Street.

"Sure." Zoey forced a smile. "I can go as soon as I finish the floor, if you'd like."

"Whatever works best for you, sweetheart."

To get the errand over with as quickly as possible, that's what worked best, Zoey thought. Before she could change her mind, she asked the question that she didn't want to ask.

"Can you think of anything else you'd like me to do while I'm out and about?" If Gran needed a prescription refilled or cream for her morning coffee, Zoey preferred to accomplish everything in one trip.

Liz tipped her head. "Come to think of it, there *is* something else. Did I mention that I've been the choir director at Church of the Pines for the past few years?"

"No, you didn't." But Zoey wasn't surprised—her grandmother had a beautiful voice. She remembered Liz singing praise songs as she worked around the house. Grandpa Jonathan would whistle along, enthusiastic but off-key.

"Every day is a celebration," Liz would say. "You can always find a reason to praise God."

On the outside, Zoey had rolled her eyes. What she hadn't realized was that on the inside, the words had been planted like seeds in her soul, lying dormant until the right conditions caused them to sprout.

"Diana Riggs took over the choir while I was in the hospital, but she's going out of town for the weekend. She knows I like to tie in the songs with Matthew's sermon." Zoey braced herself, knowing what was coming next. She knew, she just *knew,* that Gran's second errand would somehow involve Matt. "She asked if I'd look over the music she selected for this Sunday's service."

"No problem." Zoey tried to hide her relief. "Where does Diana live?"

"Oh, the music isn't at her house. She left it at the church, along with Matthew's sermon notes. Do you mind stopping by and picking them up?"

Yes.

"No," Zoey said weakly. "Of course not."

"Wonderful." Gran's response was much more enthusiastic.

"I'll have a pot of tea ready by the time you get back."

Fifteen minutes later, Zoey shrugged on her navy-blue pea coat and was on her way out the door. The temperature had slowly crept into the upper forties so she decided to take her grandmother's advice and walk downtown instead of drive.

Mirror Lake hadn't changed much from what she could see. Like many other small communities in the northern part of the state, it had flourished during the lumber era but gradually dwindled in size and population. But local pride ran as deep as the roots of the towering pine trees. The town's turn-of-the-century charm had been preserved in the sturdy brick buildings that lined both sides of Main Street. Businesses catered more to locals than the tourists who kept to the main highways. The lake itself wasn't large enough to appeal to people who wanted a vacation spot that offered more than beautiful sunsets and a quiet place to fish.

There were no fast-food restaurants. No shopping malls.

As a teenager, Zoey had thought it was the end of nowhere.

A mission school in Africa had seemed more appealing at the time, if her parents would have agreed to take her with them.

Zoey tried to shake the thought away, but it clung like a burr to her soul. It had been the final rejection. Her parents leaving her in Mirror Lake.

They'd claimed it was for the best, but Zoey knew the truth. The decision had been the best one for *them*. She'd disappointed them in so many ways, she didn't blame them for not wanting to deal with her anymore.

Zoey had vowed to make them sorry for leaving

her behind, but in the end she was the one who had been sorry.

The bell above the door of the variety store announced her arrival and brought a woman rushing out of the back room.

"Can I help you find something?" The smile was friendly. The face unfamiliar.

"I'm looking for the yarn." Zoey's hands fisted inside of her coat pockets.

"Second aisle, all the way down on your left. If you need help, just give me a holler."

"Thank you." Zoey quickly retreated as two more customers came in, stomping the slush from their shoes as they chatted.

She located the craft section and glanced at the length of yarn tied around her wrist in order to find its match on the shelf.

"Did you hear that Decker girl is back in town?"

Zoey froze as the two women who had come into the store made their way down the next aisle. She couldn't see their faces, but their voices carried through the shelves that separated them.

"I can't believe she'd even show her face in Mirror Lake again. Especially after what she did."

"Apparently she moved back in with her grandmother. You'd think Liz would know better."

"It sure didn't work out the last time she tried it."

"I heard that Liz just got out the hospital a few days ago. Maybe she doesn't feel well enough to show her the door."

"Well, hopefully someone's keeping an eye on Liz. To make sure she doesn't get taken advantage of..."

The conversation faded as the women turned down another aisle.

Until now, Zoey hadn't realized how much she'd been holding onto the hope that time and distance might have softened peoples' hearts. Changed their perspective a little.

But then again, why should it? She still carried the memory of the accident with her every single day.

Tucking two skeins of yarn under her arm, Zoey hurried up to the cash register before the women finished their shopping and circled back to the front of the store.

The woman behind the counter, however, seemed determined to prolong the transaction. "This shade of green is very pretty. What are you going to make with it?"

"I don't knit. I'm buying the yarn for someone else." Zoey resisted the urge to scoot around the counter and ring up the purchase herself.

"Did you see the coupon in the newspaper this week? With a ten dollar purchase, you get a free votive candle."

"I don't have a coupon..."

"Don't worry about that," the clerk said cheerfully. "I always put a few extra aside, just for customers like you...somewhere." She began to sift through a sheaf of loose papers on the counter.

"That's all right." A note of desperation crept into

Zoey's voice. "You can save the coupon for someone else."

The two women rounded the aisle and paused for a moment in front of the candy bar display.

"Here it is!" A colorful strip of paper spun across the counter. "Now, I'll just need some information for our mailing list. What is your name?"

"Zoey Decker." Zoey kept her voice low.

"Oh! Are you by any chance related to Liz Decker?" The clerk's eyes brightened with curiosity.

The women behind her stopped chatting. And Zoey was suddenly struck from behind by an invisible wave of disapproval.

"She's my grandmother."

"I know Liz." The clerk's smile widened. "When my husband and I moved here last year, she invited us to church. She's a very special lady. You're blessed to call her family."

"I know." If only Gran could say the same thing about her.

"Your total is ten dollars and fifty-three cents. You can choose your favorite color—"

"Here you go." Zoey paid for the yarn, snatched up a yellow candle and fled.

"Matthew!" Liz put down the magazine she'd been thumbing through with a smile of delight. "I didn't expect to see you this afternoon."

"I had to pick up something at home and thought I'd

stop in and say hello." Matt leaned down and planted a kiss on Liz's cheek.

"Sit down for a few minutes." Liz patted the spot next to her on the velvet sofa. "I was just reading. Again."

"You love to read."

"Only when I don't have to."

"I never knew you were such a rebel." Matt adjusted one of the pillows before sitting down.

"It's classified information." Liz's eyes twinkled.

"Your secrets are safe with me." Matt settled back against the cushions and studied the color in the older woman's cheeks, relieved to see that Liz appeared more well rested than she had in weeks.

Liz scooted a plate of cookies on the coffee table closer to him. "I know that."

Matt regarded her steadily. "Then why didn't you ever mention a granddaughter?"

The laughter in Liz's eyes faded as if a curtain had been drawn over them.

"I might not have talked about Zoey, but I never stopped praying for her," she said after a long pause. "Sometimes things happen that are too painful to talk about with anyone but the Lord. Some people we hold so close in our hearts that it becomes difficult to share them.

"You're young," she continued. The words were said with a hint of envy rather than condescension. "I know you might not understand that."

Matt felt a hitch in his breathing as an image of his former girlfriend Kristen's face rose in his mind.

Unfortunately, he understood all too well. No one but his college roommate knew what had happened between him and Kristen. Matt pushed the memory aside. This was about Liz, not him.

"But you're all right with Zoey being here?" He had to ask.

"Zoey being here is an answer to prayer," Liz said simply.

Matt couldn't argue with that. He'd been praying for Liz, too. He just hadn't expected a young woman with a captivating smile and eyes filled with secrets to be the answer.

Chapter Seven

"Pastor! Do you have a minute?" Kate Nichols leaned out the door of the Grapevine, waving a white dish towel to get Matt's attention.

Matt glanced both ways before he crossed the street, more out of habit than concern for traffic. Once school let out for the day, a person could practically shoot a cannon down Main Street and not hit anything.

"Is everything all right?" Something told Matt that this time, the color in Kate's cheeks hadn't come from working over a hot griddle.

"Abby called a little while ago and it seems she's having a bit of a family…situation," Kate explained breathlessly.

Matt frowned. "What's going on?"

Abby Porter, who had opened a bed and breakfast on Mirror Lake the summer before, was fairly new to his congregation, but Matt already counted her and her fiancé, Quinn O'Halloran, as good friends.

Quinn owned a local security company and volunteered with the mentoring ministry Church of the Pines had started for boys from single-parent families.

"Abby is fine," Kate huffed. "It's the wedding plans that are the problem."

"Planning a wedding can be stressful."

"Especially if the wedding involves a bossy big brother."

"Alex has been voicing his opinion again?"

"That's a nice way of putting it." Kate scowled. "I told Abby that I would stop over after work today to provide a little moral support, but then I remembered that I promised Liz Decker a piece of pecan pie today. I'll throw in an extra one for you if you don't mind playing delivery boy."

"That's not necessary." Having an excuse to see Zoey again was incentive enough.

Not that he planned to share that bit of information with Kate.

Since his move to Mirror Lake, he'd become the target of more than one well-meaning matchmaker. Not only did the members of his congregation want to feed him, it appeared that they also wanted to see him happily married and settled down with a family.

There'd only been one woman Matt had asked to share his life.

For the second time in less than an hour, he thought about Kristen.

Matt drew in a careful breath, wondering if there

would ever come a time when the memory of that brief college romance would no longer feel like a knife sliding between his ribs.

Not even his closest friends knew about his relationship with Kristen. It was a hurt Matt kept well hidden, but it was always there. Like a bruise just below the surface of the skin.

"If it's a problem…"

Matt realized that Kate had misunderstood the reason for his lengthy silence. "No, it's not a problem. And please let Abby know that I'm praying for her."

"Pray for Alex Porter, too," Kate suggested tartly, not disguising her dislike for Abby's brother. "Because if our paths ever cross, he's going to need it."

Matt grinned, not doubting it for a minute.

He followed Kate into the café, and she disappeared through the swinging doors that separated the dining area from the kitchen.

The supper crowd hadn't descended on the cafe yet. A group of teenagers huddled together in a corner booth, sharing an order of fries. At a table to Matt's right, two women he didn't recognize were involved in a heated discussion. Because they made no attempt to lower their voices, Matt couldn't help but overhear the conversation.

"The Curtises had to move away from Mirror Lake. Their *home*," one of the women was saying. "Because of her."

"I know. It isn't fair," her companion agreed. "Especially since she went right along on her merry way."

"No consequences whatsoever."

"She's only going to stir up more trouble. Wait and see."

A disdainful snort followed the observation. "From what I've heard, trouble is what she excelled at…"

The women fell silent as Kate bounded out of the kitchen.

"Here you go. It's still too warm to cut, so you'll just have to take the whole thing." She transferred a whole pie into Matt's hands. "I'm sure Liz will share."

"Thanks, Kate."

Matt's smile faded as he stepped outside. Fragments of the conversation he'd overheard began to cycle through his mind.

Caused enough damage.

No consequences.

He had no idea who they had been gossiping about, but he did know one thing. Some of what the woman had said wasn't true.

A person's mistakes always resulted in consequences, even if no one could see them on the outside.

That was another thing Matt's relationship with Kristen had taught him.

Zoey blinked back the tears that blurred her vision. She tried to think of an excuse—any excuse—she could give Gran as to why she couldn't stop by the church. But because she couldn't think of a single one, she had no choice but to move forward.

What she really wanted to do was jump into her car and drive back to Lake Delton.

The conversation Zoey overheard in the variety store had left her shaken. The women's open animosity allowing doubt and discouragement to seep in again.

As a teenager, her arrival had been cause for gossip and speculation. Now, it was happening all over again. All she'd wanted to do was help her grandmother but not if her presence was going to do more harm than good.

Even if she left earlier than she'd planned, Liz would be well taken care of. She had the knitting group. And her church family.

And Matt.

"You are a wise woman, Zoey Decker."

He had sounded so certain of it that, for a moment, Zoey had felt a tiny flicker of hope. Hope that Matt would see her as more than the sum of her past mistakes...

Don't even think about it. Don't think about him.

She would stay through the weekend, accompany Gran to her appointment with Dr. Parish on Monday and then go back to Lake Delton, where she belonged.

Because she didn't belong in Mirror Lake. She never had.

As Zoey stepped into the church, the scent of lemon polish and sunshine rolled over her, stirring up another batch of bittersweet memories.

"Hello?" Zoey peeked into the first office at the end of the hall. The lights were on, but there was no sign of the church secretary. The one adjacent to it was also dark. Matt must have gone out for the day.

At least now she could honestly tell Gran that she'd tried.

Zoey paused as she reached the doors leading to the sanctuary.

Late-afternoon sunshine streamed through the stained glass windows, creating jewel-like stencils on the gleaming hardwood floor. The old-fashioned pews were arranged in neat rows, just the way she remembered.

As a teenager, Zoey had resisted going to church, certain that everyone was watching her—waiting for her to make a mistake. She hadn't realized that by keeping people at arm's length to protect herself, she had distanced herself from God, too. The only one who had the power to heal the damaged places in her heart.

And because her heart felt as if it had been stomped on again, Zoey nudged the door open and took refuge inside.

On his way back to church, Matt took a shortcut through the park. The old-fashioned steeple rising above the maple trees guided him like a compass. The sun felt warmer today, and the breeze that ruffled his hair carried the earthy scent of spring.

Some people complained about the long winters,

but they only made Matt appreciate spring even more. The changes were so small, so subtle, that it sometimes seemed as if winter would never relax its grip. But they were there. A lot like the hand of God working behind the scenes of his own life.

Two years in Mirror Lake had strengthened Matt's faith in astonishing ways.

While attending seminary, Matt had heard some of his fellow classmates express their desire to pastor large churches. Ones that had the space, and members, to offer a wide variety of ministries.

Matt hadn't cared about any of that. He'd reached a point in his life where his plans no longer mattered. The best place to be was the place where God put him.

Not that he hadn't been a little taken aback when he'd arrived in Mirror Lake and saw his new church for the first time.

It looked like one of the country churches a person might see on the front of a Christmas card, right down to the wide double doors, white clapboard siding and stained glass windows.

But what the building lacked in size, the people more than made up for in warmth.

It was one of the reasons why Delia's reaction to the news of Zoey's arrival had been a little unsettling.

Balancing the pie in the crook of one arm, Matt pushed his shoulder against the door. Cheryl left early on Friday afternoons, so the building was quiet except for the soft, uneven purr of the furnace.

Matt set the pie down on a bench in the foyer and padded down the hall to make sure everything was locked up. As he walked past the doors leading to the sanctuary, something caught his eye.

Or rather, someone.

A slight figure sat motionless at the piano. Even though Matt couldn't see the person's face, he recognized the shoulder-length hair with its cherry-cola highlights.

Zoey.

What was she doing here?

Matt hesitated, not wanting to intrude. People generally retreated to the sanctuary when they wanted to be alone, but something in the forlorn slump of her shoulders propelled him to her side.

"Hey."

Zoey's head jerked up. Matt was stunned to see the diamond-bright sheen of tears in her eyes before she looked away.

The sudden urge to put his arms around her—to shelter her from hurt—was so strong that he jammed his hands into his pockets so he wouldn't act on it. Zoey was skittish around him already.

He slid onto the bench beside her instead. "This is great. I always hoped that one day I would get a chance to impress someone with my skills. Are you ready?" He didn't wait for her to respond but flexed his fingers and attacked the ivory keys.

By the time the song ended, Zoey was staring at him in amazement. And trying not to smile.

"Well?" Matt leaned back. "What did you think?"

"That was…Chopsticks."

He gave her a look. "I'll have you know it was more than Chopsticks. What you just witnessed was the culmination of six months of piano lessons."

"Six *months?*" Zoey echoed.

Matt leaned closer, and the scent of her perfume stirred his senses. A tantalizing floral blend as sweet—and complex—as the woman who wore it. "That's how long it took for my dad to pull me aside and offer me twenty-five dollars if I'd never play again."

Zoey's laughter rippled through the room.

Mission accomplished.

"Would you like to try?" Matt smiled down at her.

"No," Zoey said promptly. "I'm pretty sure that I can't do what you just did."

"It's easy," he persisted. "Put your fingers here." Matt tapped the ivory keys.

"Those who can't do, teach?" she ventured.

He pressed a hand against his broad chest and reeled back. "Ouch."

A smile played at the corners of Zoey's lips as she rested her fingers on the keys. "Like this?"

"Very good." Matt's serious expression belied the gleam of laughter in his eyes. "You'll have it down in no time."

Zoey didn't have the heart to admit that she'd been

playing the piano since the age of seven. "That's true. Look what you accomplished in six months."

He grinned. "Maybe I missed my calling."

His calling.

The reminder of who he was—and what he did for a living— washed over her like a spray of ice water. At the same time, the sound of a door opening registered.

Zoey surged to her feet. "Did you hear that? I think someone is here."

"Whoever it is will find us," Matt said mildly.

She shot him a look that was half frustrated, half pleading.

That's what Zoey was afraid of.

Matt had no idea what kind of situation he was placing himself in by being seen with her. Alone. It would only add to the rumors that were probably already spreading through town. She'd damaged her own reputation—the last thing she wanted to do was cast a shadow on his.

"I should go," she murmured. "I don't want to leave Gran alone for very long."

Matt put his hand on her arm. "I'm sure you didn't stop by for a piano lesson…"

Zoey blushed. A few minutes in his company and she'd totally forgotten the reason she'd stopped by the church in the first place.

"Gran asked if I would pick up your sermon notes along with the music for Sunday's service."

Something—it couldn't have been disappointment?— flashed in Matt's eyes. He didn't think she had stopped by to see…him?

Like a crocus pushing its way out of the frozen ground, hope slipped through a crack in Zoey's defenses.

Did he enjoy spending time with her?

Or was he simply being kind? Doing what he was paid to do?

"The notes are in my office," Matt was saying. "And if you don't mind hanging around for a few minutes, I'll walk you home."

Home.

For a split second, Zoey savored the word like a piece of dark chocolate.

"Is anyone here?" A voice drifted down the hallway. Jerked her back to reality.

"You should see who it is." Zoey inched further away from Matt. "I'll wait for you."

For a moment, she was afraid he would argue with her.

"All right." He unfolded his lean frame from the piano bench. Paused. "You won't run out on me as soon as my back is turned, will you?"

He knew her too well. Which was crazy because he barely knew her at all.

"No." Zoey didn't sound too convincing. Matt must have thought so, too.

"Promise?"

"Promise," she muttered.

The doors swished closed behind him and Zoey

stared down at the piano keys, tempted to make a break for the exit door behind the altar.

It wouldn't have been the first time she'd used it.

Would Matt still smile at her if he knew the truth?

Not for the first time, Zoey wished she could live the two years she'd spent in Mirror Lake all over again. She wouldn't have caused her grandparents so much pain.

And she never would have gotten into the car with Tyler Curtis that night.

"Zoey?" Matt appeared in the doorway, a grim look on his face. "I'm afraid this might take a while. If you don't mind going on ahead without me, I'll stop by and drop off the music and my sermon notes on the way home." He raked a hand through his hair, tousling the burnished-gold strands. "I'm sorry."

"It's all right." Maybe, Zoey thought, the interruption had been divine intervention instead. A gentle reminder that it wasn't wise to let her guard down with Matt.

Based on the little she knew about him already, he sincerely cared about people. His close relationship with God had been evident in the simple but heartfelt prayer he had spoken at supper the night before. Matt's confidence and strength, his easygoing smile and rock-solid faith, would encourage people to trust him.

Zoey felt a pang of envy even as she acknowledged

that she could never accept that kind of pressure. Not because she didn't care about people, but because she was afraid she would let them down.

Chapter Eight

"Now that is a Mona Lisa smile if I've ever seen one."

Zoey hadn't heard Gran come into the parlor. "Just…thinking."

"About what?" Liz's voice was teasing. "Or should I say about 'who'?"

"About whether I should make an extra pot of coffee for the knitting group." She tried to bluff her way through.

"Uh-huh." The sparkle in the lively brown eyes told Zoey that her grandmother didn't believe her.

"So, what do you think?" Zoey bent down and fussed with the napkins she'd arranged in a wicker basket.

Liz looked down at the array of goodies spread out on the coffee table. "I think that you shouldn't have gone to all this trouble."

"It's no trouble."

"I appreciate your effort, Zoey, but please don't feel

any pressure to make things perfect. I've known these girls forever. There's no need to impress anyone."

Zoey didn't argue. Or agree. Maybe it was true that Gran didn't need to impress anyone, but the only thing people knew about her was the heartache she'd caused. Not only to her grandparents, but to the entire town.

Which once again prompted Zoey to wish that she could take back her impulsive offer to host Gran's knitting group. As long as she could retreat to her bedroom and wait it out, though, she would be fine.

"I think everything's ready." Zoey took one last look at the table. "I'll be in my room catching up on some reading." She had brought along the script for the play so she could practice her lines during her absence, but she hadn't had an opportunity to glance through it yet.

"Are you sure?" Disappointment clouded Liz's eyes.

Zoey didn't pretend to misunderstand. "I don't want to ruin your evening."

Gran squeezed her hand. "You wouldn't ruin it, sweetheart, but I won't push. Not tonight anyway," she added with a mischievous smile.

Zoey chuckled. "Thanks for the warning."

The sound of the door opening, along with a sudden chorus of cheerful greetings, sent Zoey's heart into a tailspin. Apparently the knitting group didn't feel compelled to knock before making their entrance.

"I'll come down later, Gran. After everyone leaves."
Zoey practically sprinted toward the stairway.

And almost made it.

"Zoey?"

At the sound of her name, Zoey's feet froze on the
stairs.

She turned around slowly, knowing it would be
rude to ignore the lilting voice and continue her mad
dash to safety.

A trio of women close to her own age stood at the
bottom of the stairs, looking up at her. Two of them
were strangers, but Zoey recognized the petite redhead in the middle.

Kate Nichols had been out of high school for several years by the time Zoey arrived in Mirror Lake,
but she remembered her from the Grapevine, a favorite hangout for the local teenagers. Kate's parents had
owned the tiny diner, where she'd filled in as both
short-order cook and waitress on the weekends.

Zoey's heart dropped. "Hi, Kate."

"I heard you were back."

Of course she had.

Unsure of how to respond, Zoey sidled up another
step. "Gran is waiting in the parlor."

Before she could escape, the slender, tawny-haired
young woman on Kate's right bounded up the stairs
and extended her hand. "I'm Abby Porter."

"Zoey Decker."

"It's great to meet you." Abby smiled as if she
meant it.

"Nice to meet you, too," Zoey mumbled, a little taken aback by the warmth of the greeting.

"I'm new in town, too," Abby said.

That explained it, then. Abby Porter hadn't connected the name Zoey Decker with the tragedy that had rocked the small town.

She spared a glance at Kate, surprised to find her expression still as open and friendly as Zoey remembered.

"And this is Emma Sutton." Kate made the introduction for the other woman standing next to her. "Zoey Decker is Liz's granddaughter."

If that was the only thing Zoey was known for, she would be content.

"Hello." Emma flashed a shy but pleasant smile. "Delia mentioned that you were going to be our hostess for the evening."

Zoey tried not to cringe.

What else had Delia said?

"Not the hostess," she denied. "I just put on a pot of coffee." She glanced at Kate. "Actually, Kate provided the dessert."

"Pie, right?" Abby crossed her arms. "Just to show me up."

Zoey blinked.

"Abby bought the old Bible camp on the lake and turned it into a bed and breakfast last summer." Kate's shamrock-green eyes sparkled with laughter. She lowered her voice in a stage whisper. "She's a phenomenal cook, but my pies are better."

Abby nodded, not at all offended by the claim. "I'm trying to talk her into supplying the desserts for the inn. She claims that she's too busy, but I never take no for an answer."

"Neither does Kate," Emma murmured.

Both women smiled smugly, as if she had given them a compliment.

"Well, have fun." Zoey hoped they would take the hint.

"Aren't you going to join us?" Abby asked.

"Me?" Zoey's eyes widened. "I don't knit."

And even though these three women didn't look at her as if she were a stain on their best sweater, Zoey wasn't ready to face Delia Peake and the rest of Gran's friends from Church of the Pines.

"That makes four of us then," Kate said cheerfully. "You'd be in good company. We're the newest members of the Knit-Our-Hearts-Together group." She shifted her weight to model the canvas tote draped over her shoulder. The light from the chandelier bounced off a pair of metallic-green knitting needles poking out of the top.

"I just joined last fall," Emma chimed in. "I'm working on a scarf for my husband's birthday, but at the rate it's going, it will have to be a Christmas present instead."

"I thought it was supposed to be a wedding gift." Kate grinned.

Emma blushed but didn't deny it.

"Emma and Jake got married a few months ago,"

Abby explained. "Technically, she's still on her honeymoon."

Zoey's fingers curled around the banister for support. "I don't think—"

"At least give it a try," Kate interrupted. "I'm sure Liz has some needles and yarn you can borrow."

"And if you don't like to knit, you can always eat pie," Abby interjected.

Zoey sighed. Apparently Emma was right. They weren't going to take no for an answer.

Half an hour later, Zoey wished they had.

The knitting group had grown in membership over the years, but Zoey recognized many of the women who crowded into the parlor. Gran took a moment at the beginning of the meeting to introduce her, but judging from the expressions on the women's faces, which ranged from mild disapproval to outright hostility, it hadn't been necessary.

Zoey could almost read their thoughts. Ten years ago, what was supposed to have been a day of celebration had turned into a day of mourning instead. Because of her.

Rose Williams, who arrived a few minutes late, looked ready to walk out when she spotted Zoey sitting by the fireplace. If Esther Redstone hadn't waved her over and pointed to an empty chair, Zoey had no doubt the woman would have stormed out rather than spend an hour in the same room with her.

Rose and Tyler Curtis's mother had been close friends and even though the rest of the group had settled in and started to work on their projects, Zoey could still feel the woman's glare across the room.

If only she could come up with an excuse to leave...

"It's okay," Abby whispered, the look of compassion in her eyes making Zoey wonder if she was talking about the knitting project. "You're doing great."

Kate leaned closer and studied the row of knots tightly coiled around Zoey's knitting needle. "She's right. You're getting the hang of it."

"It's much better than my first attempt," Emma agreed with a smile.

Zoey's eyes stung. She hadn't expected this, especially when none of her so-called "friends" had stood up for her after the accident. But Kate, Emma and Abby seemed oblivious to the fact that reaching out to her might somehow damage their own standing in the group. Instead, they had positioned themselves around her, creating a human buffer between Zoey and the disapproving looks and occasional whispered comment.

Kate reached for the coffee carafe and frowned. "I think it's empty—again."

"I'll get some more." Zoey almost snatched it from Kate's hand in her haste to escape for a few minutes. While she put another pot on to brew, she began to straighten up the kitchen.

"You can drop the act now. No one is watching."

Zoey glanced over her shoulder and saw Rose Williams framed in the doorway. "Act?"

Her confusion must have shown because Rose rolled her eyes. "The helpful, attentive granddaughter act," she clarified. "Liz has been proudly telling everyone that you're an actress, but she doesn't seem to realize that makes her look just as naive as she was years ago—and you more trouble, if that's possible. I can't believe you have the nerve to show your face in Mirror Lake again."

Zoey met her gaze. "I'm here to help."

Something flickered in Rose's eyes and then her expression hardened. "You don't exactly have a reputation for being honest, though, do you?"

Zoey opened her mouth but then closed it again. She wanted to try and convince Rose to believe her, but she couldn't.

Because Rose was right.

She'd hidden the truth before.

Rose's eyes narrowed. "If you really want to help, you'll—"

"Oh, she's already been a great help," a quiet voice interrupted.

Zoey's heart skipped a beat as Matt sauntered in.

"Pastor Wilde." Rose Williams's smile stretched so tight Matt was sure it would snap off and ricochet around the room.

"Hello, Mrs. Williams." Matt glanced at Zoey. He wasn't sure what was going on, but whatever it was, she looked as wilted as a wildflower in the aftermath of a storm. "I'm sorry I'm late dropping off my sermon notes. I didn't want to disturb the meeting, so I thought I'd sneak in and leave them on the table."

"You two know each other?" Rose squawked.

"No." Zoey shook her head at the same time Matt nodded.

"Yes."

The contradictory statements collided in midair. Matt grinned, but Rose didn't look amused. Not at all.

"I see," she said stiffly.

Matt took a step forward and Zoey pedaled backward until she bumped against the counter. "He lives next door."

Matt wasn't sure if it was his imagination, but it looked like she was tempted to apologize for that. "Right," he said cheerfully. "That means we're neighbors."

"Neighbors." Rose's lips compressed to a stern hyphen.

Matt couldn't figure it out. On several occasions, Rose had hopped on the matchmaking bandwagon and hinted that she would love to see him settle down with a "nice Christian woman." Here he was, standing less than five feet away from what Matt thought would be a perfect woman for the woman's "list" of possible candidates and Rose looked as if Zoey didn't have a right to be in the same room with him.

"I'll be sure to give your notes to Gran," Zoey said.

Matt took the hint, although he was reluctant to

leave the two women alone. "Thanks for passing this on to Liz." He handed Zoey the manila envelope. "And let her know that if she sees any mistakes in my sermon, she should let me know. I have a reputation to uphold, you know."

He smiled to let Zoey know that he was teasing, but Rose was the one who responded.

"You're right. A person's reputation is very important."

She was looking at Zoey when she said it.

Chapter Nine

Matt's lungs were burning.

He ignored the pain as he rounded the corner, feeling the muscles in his calves contract in protest. Ordinarily he ran five miles every other weekday, taking a circular route around the lake. This morning, he'd already put in six. On a Saturday.

After he'd become a Christian, Matt had tried to pray in a quiet room because he thought it was the "right" way to connect with the Lord, but he had discovered that he felt closer to God while running down a quiet backwoods road. Over time, Matt's prayers had begun to merge with the landscape. Familiar landmarks sparked a prayer for a specific person or situation.

A fieldstone wall, constructed by early settlers, inspired a prayer for strength and endurance. The cluster of knee-high aspen trees that sprouted in the shade of a sugar maple, the mentoring ministry. A towering white pine, its bark scorched by lightning, reminded him to pray for those who were hurting.

This morning his thoughts—and his prayers—centered around a certain woman with eyes that changed color like the surface of the lake and a husky laugh that lingered in his mind like a favorite song.

Zoey was the reason he'd crawled out of bed at five o'clock and reached for his sweats.

Matt skidded to a stop when he reached the place they'd met. An oil spot marked the spot where a rusty Jeep had been parked.

Lord, I don't know what's going on with Zoey, but you do. Comfort her. Remind her that you love her.

Matt's eyes snapped open at the sound of an approaching car. He stepped onto the shoulder of the road, but instead of passing him, it cruised to a stop.

Matt glanced over his shoulder and recognized the driver as the window of the squad car scrolled down.

"Saturday morning?" Jake Sutton drawled. "What's the occasion?"

"Does everyone know my routine?" Matt complained.

"I'm sure I saw it posted on the community calendar."

Matt chuckled. "Isn't Saturday morning a change in your routine, too?"

"I'm covering for Steve Patterson," Jake explained. "His wife went into labor during the night."

"I thought in those types of situations, the police chief is supposed to call in one of his officers and go back to sleep." It was a standing joke between the two men. What Matt liked to refer to as their "on call, 24/8" lives.

"I don't mind helping out for a few hours." Jake's broad shoulders lifted in a shrug. "I promised to be home by nine. With donuts."

Matt grinned. "You're perpetuating the cliché, you know."

"They're for Emma and Jeremy." A half smile softened the stern line of Jake's jaw.

Matt felt an unexpected twinge of envy. The police chief, a former undercover drug officer, was known for being reserved. But when it came to his new family, his feelings were right there on the surface for everyone to see.

Matt had performed the couple's wedding ceremony in January. There hadn't been a dry eye in the sanctuary when Jeremy Barlow, Emma's eleven-year-old son from her first marriage, had walked his mother up the aisle.

Matt stepped back. "In that case, I better let you get to work. I'll see you tomorrow morning."

"Do you want a ride into town?"

"That would be cheating."

"It would also be faster."

At the moment, faster looked good. Faster meant that he could stop by Liz's house and beg a cup of coffee. And see Zoey again.

"You talked me into it." Matt jogged around to the passenger side of the squad car and got in.

Jake gave him a sidelong glance. "That was easy."

"I have to stop by Liz's and pick up my sermon notes for tomorrow."

"How is she doing?"

Matt gave him a sharp look. There was a serious undercurrent in Jake's voice that made the question sound less like a casual inquiry and more like he was being interviewed.

"Better than she was a week ago."

"Mmm."

"Do you know something I don't know?" Matt was only half joking.

"I got a call a little while ago from a neighbor, asking if I could swing by and do a welfare check on Liz."

A welfare check. That seemed a little odd to Matt. "I don't think that's necessary. She has family staying with her now."

"I know. Her granddaughter, Zoey Decker. Emma mentioned meeting her last night, but I didn't think anything of it. According to the neighbor who called, there is some sort of history between the two of them. She's afraid that Zoey is going to take advantage of Liz in some way."

"That's crazy," Matt said flatly.

Jake's eyes narrowed. "Why would you say that?"

"Because I was visiting Liz when Zoey arrived. Liz was thrilled to see her."

"You have to admit the timing is a little coincidental."

"Yes. It coincides with Liz's release from the hospital."

Okay, so he sounded a little defensive. Jake must have thought so too because he frowned.

"Apparently there was some kind of estrangement in the family a few years back," Jake said carefully. "The caller didn't go into detail—"

"Really?" Matt interrupted. "I'm surprised."

That earned him another long look. "All right. I trust your judgment, Matt. What is *your* impression of Zoey?"

Matt opened his mouth and then closed it again.

What was his impression of Zoey?

Sweet. Spunky. Cautious. Caring.

Beautiful.

"So…" There was a glint of amusement in Jake's eyes, as if Matt had answered the question out loud.

Matt's face heated. "Liz is thrilled that Zoey is there. No matter what happened between them in the past, I believe that Zoey Decker's motives are good. I'm not sure that opening up old wounds would be good for either of them. If they're willing to put whatever happened behind them, why can't everyone else?"

"I wasn't planning to open up 'old wounds,'" Jake said after a moment. "But I didn't get the sense that the neighbor wanted to cause trouble. She sounded genuinely concerned about Liz."

But who was concerned about Zoey? That's what Matt wanted to know.

"Calling the police seems a little extreme, that's all." Matt was tempted to say more, but didn't want their friendship to prevent Jake from doing his job.

"Fine." Jake sighed. "Consider yourself deputized."

"What?"

"I'll back off. You're not only Liz Decker's pastor, you're also her closest neighbor. In my book, that gives you the right to keep an eye on things."

"Thanks—"

"But," Jake stopped him with a look. "If something doesn't feel right, you have to let me know. In our careers, we can't let personal feelings get in the way."

Matt nodded even as he wondered if it was too late for that.

Zoey snuggled deeper into the hollow of the mattress and stared up at the stars on the ceiling. Her eyes felt dry and gritty, a reminder that she'd been awake for more hours than she had been asleep.

Gran's cough seemed to worsen during the night. Zoey had gotten up to check on her several times, refilling her glass of water on the nightstand and adjusting the pillows so that she could breathe easier.

Liz had finally fallen asleep, but Zoey curled up

in the rocking chair next to the window, not wanting to go back to her own room until she was sure her grandmother was all right.

A long time ago, Liz had maintained a similar vigil at Zoey's bedside.

Fatigue made it impossible to battle the memories that began to rise inexorably to the surface…

The pain radiating throughout her body that made it difficult to open her eyes.

And an overwhelming sense of dread that had made her *not* want to open them.

There were still times when Zoey wished that she hadn't. Times she wished she could have remained wrapped in a cocoon of hospital blankets, dulled to the pain she was in.

And the pain she'd caused.

Only her grandparents had come to visit her. The rest of the town had been in mourning for Tyler. Zoey's parents had called but she refused to talk to them. Within twenty-four hours of her release from the hospital, Zoey had left Mirror Lake for good.

The regrets seemed to sprout like weeds. She pulled one and it seemed as if another took its place.

"You reap what you sow," her father had always said.

Up until six months ago, Zoey had taken it as a negative. Now she understood that a person could plant good things, too. Kindness. Patience. Compassion.

Zoey slid to her knees beside the bed and closed her eyes, letting God continue to transform the landscape of her life.

Half an hour later, Zoey made her way to the bedroom at the end of the hall and eased the door open.

She was about to call her grandmother's name when the blankets twitched. The tightness in Zoey's chest loosened as she backed away.

Gran had teased her the night before by asking for a "wake up call" but Zoey decided to let her sleep a while longer.

Blurry-eyed, she made her way down to the kitchen and poured a cup of coffee. Taking it to the table, she gently pushed Gran's worn leather Bible and reading glasses to the side, uncovering Matt's sermon notes in the process. All over the page, written in an uneven masculine scrawl, were various scripture references.

These were the foundation of the Sunday message?

Growing up, Zoey had seen her father's meticulous, three-point sermon notes. With a warning tacked on to each verse like a footnote.

One of the passages jumped out at her and she sucked in a breath.

Psalm 40.

She opened Gran's Bible with trembling fingers and thumbed through it. She wasn't sure which section would be the focus of Matt's sermon, but she focused her attention on the third verse.

He put a new song in my mouth, a hymn of praise to our God. Many will see and fear and put their trust in the Lord.

It was like a gentle reminder from God. An extension of the conversation they had just finished at the side of her bed.

"Thank You," she whispered.

This was the same verse that had brought her back to faith.

Six months ago, tired of the emptiness, Zoey had accepted an invitation from Melissa, one of her fellow cast mates, to attend church with her. They had had a long conversation over coffee after the service. It was a turning point in Zoey's life. The moment she'd realized that although she had walked away from God, He still loved her. He hadn't abandoned her.

Zoey remembered praying for an opportunity to reconnect with her family.

Her lips curved.

She had assumed it would happen through an email. Or a long-distance phone call.

The God that Zoey had once imagined to be stern and unapproachable definitely had a sense of humor.

"The coffee smells good." Liz appeared in the doorway, sniffing the air appreciatively. "You should have woken me. I don't usually laze away the morning in bed."

"It's only eight o'clock, Gran," Zoey pointed out with a smile as she rose to pour another cup.

Her grandmother sank into one of the straight-back chairs at the table. "I'm sorry I kept you up during the night."

"I remember giving you a few sleepless nights," Zoey said lightly. "Let's call it even."

Liz reached for her glasses and slipped them on. The Bible still lay open on the table, Matt's notes spread out beside it. She chuckled. "A little difficult to decipher, aren't they?"

Zoey blushed as if she'd been caught with her hand in the cookie jar. "I can't believe he preaches an entire sermon from a few random words written on a piece of paper. Dad's sermons ran about ten pages and he arranged each point alphabetically."

She was teasing, but Liz didn't return the smile. "I don't mean to sound critical, Zoey, but your father could only make sense of things when they were structured a certain way."

Zoey's throat tightened.

Pastor Decker liked order. In his sermons. His church. His schedule.

His daughter.

A natural move toward independence had been viewed as rebellion. A flaw in the mold everyone had expected her to fit. The older Zoey got, the more she felt the weight of peoples' expectations.

She had tried to please her parents. At their encouragement, she was involved in the youth group and performed special music for Christmas and Easter services.

The trouble had crested when Zoey auditioned for the musical her high school put on every spring. A freshman had never been chosen to play the lead female role but Zoey got the part.

Two weeks into rehearsals, Zoey's father had called her into his office. Several members of the congregation had questioned her involvement in the play, suggesting that her time would be better spent in church-related activities. Not only that, several of the teenagers came from questionable families and they *knew* that Pastor Decker wouldn't want Zoey to be spending time with kids who might have a negative influence on her.

Her father had agreed.

After that, anger and disappointment had fueled Zoey's choices. If people were going to believe the worst no matter what she did, why not do whatever she wanted?

That question had started Zoey's journey into a dark tunnel. One that had separated her from her family. And from God. For a long time, Zoey believed she would never be good enough for Him either.

"Matthew's sermons might not look organized, but they come from the heart," Liz was saying. "I knew there was something special about him the first time we met at his interview. He knows what's important."

"The church."

"People." Her grandmother smiled. "That's why everyone respects him. He accepts them right where they are."

Zoey pushed to her feet. Talking about Matt stirred up a longing that she wasn't prepared to examine too closely.

"I thought I'd run to the grocery store this morning and pick up a few things."

"Do you mind running the notes over to Matt before you leave? He practices his sermons on Saturday afternoon."

Zoey stifled a groan. Hopefully Matt would be gone and she could leave the papers in the door.

Chapter Ten

Matt's heart bounced off his rib cage when he opened the door and saw Zoey pushing an envelope into the rusty mailbox attached to it. In faded jeans and a sweatshirt that brought out a hint of blue in her pearl-gray eyes, she looked…stunning.

And startled to see him.

"You're here."

There was only one way to respond to that. And somehow, he managed to say it without stammering. "Yes."

Matt had been thinking about Zoey ever since Jake dropped him off in the squad car. Instead of knocking on Liz's door and inviting himself in for a cup of coffee, Matt had retreated to the carriage house. The conversation with the police chief had given him a lot to think—and pray—about.

Looking at Zoey, it was difficult to imagine how anyone could question her motives for moving in with Liz. There was a vulnerability about her that told Matt she wasn't the kind of person who would intentionally hurt someone. In fact, judging from the shadows he glimpsed in Zoey's eyes from time to time, Matt guessed that *she* was the one who'd been hurt.

"I thought you were gone…" Zoey caught herself when his eyebrow shot up. "I mean, I didn't see your truck parked in the driveway."

"A friend of mine borrowed it for the day."

"Oh." Zoey thrust a handful of papers toward him that Matt recognized as his sermon notes. "Gran finished looking these over and she mentioned that you need them to practice your sermon."

"Your timing is good." Matt stepped to the side. "I have something for her, too. One of the members of the congregation dropped it off here last night because they noticed Liz had company and didn't want to intrude. I was going to stop over later, so you saved me a trip."

After a moment's hesitation, Zoey followed him inside.

Matt was glad he'd taken a few minutes to straighten up the place but it wasn't exactly *Better Homes and Gardens* quality. He saw Zoey's gaze slide to the breakfast dishes that formed a semi-circle around his Bible.

She stopped just inside the doorway, a clear sign that she was anxious to be on her way. But now that she was here, Matt was reluctant to let her go.

"Does the carriage house look the way you remember it?" he asked.

Zoey shook her head. "Grandpa used it for storage when I lived here. I remember peeking in the windows and seeing old bicycles. Gardening tools. Stuff like that."

When I lived here.

As tempted as he was to take advantage of the opening she'd just given him, Matt hadn't invited her in for an interrogation.

Some deputy he was turning out to be. Jake would take away his badge.

"Daniel Redstone, one of the men in the congregation, did most of the remodeling." Matt looked around, trying to see the place through Zoey's eyes. Most of the furnishings were secondhand, overflow from peoples' generosity—and attics. The result was an eclectic blend that suited a bachelor who spent more time at the church than he did his home. "I have a list of things I'd like to do eventually, but..."

"But right now you're helping other people cross off the things on their lists," Zoey finished the sentence.

He gave her a lopsided smile. "Right." He saw her attention settle on a bouquet of daisies sprouting from a vase in the middle of the coffee table.

"That's what I'm supposed to give you. Brenda hoped they would brighten Liz's day a little."

"Gran loves fresh flowers."

"How is she feeling this morning?"

"She was awake a few times during the night," Zoey

admitted. "The medication she's taking is supposed to be helping her cough, but it still sounds bad."

Matt noticed the smudges under Zoey's eyes. Apparently Liz wasn't the only one who hadn't slept. Struck by a sudden, inexplicable urge to draw her into his arms, Matt pushed his hands into the pockets of his jeans instead.

If you want to cheer her up, you better stick to Chopsticks.

"When is Liz's next appointment with Dr. Parish?"

Zoey didn't answer. She was staring at something behind him.

Matt followed her gaze and saw the enormous calico cat curled up in his leather recliner. The most comfortable chair in the house. They battled over the territory every day so it came down to whoever got there first. Matt usually lost.

"Oh, that's my roommate. Not that we negotiated a contract or anything. When I moved in, so did she."

Zoey didn't seem to be listening. She crossed the room and perched gingerly on the edge of the chair. Lime-green eyes rolled open to check out the disturbance.

"Careful. She's kind of cranky…" Matt's warning died in his throat. To his amazement, the ordinarily standoffish animal stretched out her front paws and pushed her wedge-shaped face against Zoey's hand.

"Hey there," Zoey crooned, gathering the cat into her lap.

"Don't laugh, but she has a weird name for a female cat. It's—"

"George."

Matt stared at her. "How did you know that?"

"Because I named her," Zoey whispered. "Grandpa gave her to me on my seventeenth birthday. She was just a kitten. I named her after a character in a book." She was staring down at the cat as if she were afraid it would disappear. "I didn't know that...I was afraid to ask Gran what had happened to her." Zoey wrapped her arms around the cat, which jumpstarted a chainsaw-like purr.

George could *purr?*

He'd had no idea.

Just like he'd had no idea that for the past two years, he'd been taking care of Zoey's cat.

"Why didn't you take her with you when you left?"

Zoey didn't answer right away. "I thought she'd be better off here."

The shadows had returned, dimming the light in her expressive eyes like an evening mist. Matt wanted nothing more than to chase them away. "I think she remembers you."

"Really?" Hope and doubt battled for dominance in Zoey's eyes.

"I don't think I've ever heard her purr before. To tell you the truth, I think it's the recliner she likes, not necessarily my company." Matt reached down and rubbed his knuckles against the soft fur between

George's ears. "But she is the first one who hears my sermons. Every Saturday afternoon."

A smile shimmered in Zoey's eyes.

A smile that stalled his heart in midbeat.

Matt swallowed.

"She used to curl up on the end of my bed and listen to me sing," Zoey admitted softly. "She never cared about what song it was either."

Matt read between the lines.

Someone had.

Matt realized that he had just been given a gift. A brief, unguarded glimpse into Zoey's heart.

He nodded, feeling his way through uncharted territory. Afraid that one careless word would send her running for cover again. "I know what you mean. George never falls asleep in the middle of my sermons. And she's never critical."

Zoey's laughter bubbled up like a spring. "Or it could be that George is hard of hearing. She is getting up there in cat years, you know."

"Hey." Matt grinned, thrilled that she'd let her guard down long enough to tease him.

"Dad always practiced his sermons on me," Zoey said after a moment.

It was the first time she had mentioned her father. "He must have valued your opinion."

Pain flashed across Zoey's face like summer lightning. "Not really." Her smile, when it appeared, was rueful. "I think he wanted to make sure I heard them twice."

Matt tried to remember what Liz had said about her only son and his wife. "Your parents are on the mission field. In Africa, right?"

"Yes."

"So, how many years did you live over there?" Matt asked, then instantly regretted asking the question. He could see Zoey shut down. It was like watching a castle come under siege. Bolts in place. Windows slammed shut. Doors barred.

"I better go. I promised Gran I'd make a grocery store run today." Zoey gently moved George off her lap.

She'd retrieved the bouquet of daisies and was half-way to the door before Matt realized it. He scooped up a boneless, purring George and followed.

"Wait a second. You forgot something."

Zoey turned around and her eyes widened. "Matt, no—" Her voice barely rose above a whisper. "She belongs to you now."

Ignoring her protest, Matt transferred the cat into her arms. "Say 'welcome home.'"

"Welcome home," Zoey murmured, pressing her cheek against the soft ruff of fur below the cat's whiskers.

Matt felt a hitch in his breathing. "I was talking to George."

"I can't believe that cat is back again." Gran chuckled as George trotted into the room at Zoey's heels, her feather duster tail swishing the air.

"You don't mind, do you?" Zoey asked anxiously.

"Of course not," came the instant reply. "George was good company until Matt moved in next door." Liz chuckled. "She would climb onto his lap when he came over for a visit. The next thing I knew, George was spending more time at the carriage house than she was with me. I teased Matt that he lured her away with kitty treats. He was new in town, though, and didn't really know anyone. He needed her more."

It was so like Liz to put someone else's needs before her own, but Zoey doubted that her grandmother was right. A man like Matt wouldn't be lonely. Not with a congregation of a hundred people looking out for him.

And even though Zoey was pretty sure Matt had been joking when he'd confessed that George was the first one who heard his sermons, he hadn't laughed at her when she admitted that the cat had once been her confidante, too.

Matt's expression had softened and, for a brief moment, they had shared a connection. It was as if he understood the importance of having someone to talk to. Someone who didn't judge your every thought and action. Who didn't care that you weren't perfect…

Zoey shook the thought away.

She couldn't imagine anyone being critical of Matt. Why would they be? He had never hurt anyone.

Matt didn't have to live every day with the consequences of a youthful mistake.

"Do you think George would rather be with Matt?

I could take her back." Maybe Matt already regretted his decision to return George to her former owner. After all, Zoey had admitted that she'd abandoned the animal once before.

Liz glanced down at George, draped around Zoey's ankles like a luxurious feather boa. "I think she'll wear a path between here and the carriage house. You and Matthew might have to share custody."

The thought of sharing anything with Matt sent a shiver up Zoey's arms.

She deliberately steered the conversation to safer ground.

"Did you need anything before I turn in for the night, Gran?"

"Yes, as a matter of fact I could use your opinion." Liz opened the closet doors and pulled out two blouses. "Which one do you like better?"

"The yellow one," Zoey said promptly. "It reminds me of spring."

"I think so, too." Liz hung the pink shirt back in the closet and draped the yellow one over the back of a chair. "Now, we're all set."

"All set for what?"

"For church tomorrow."

"You're going to church?" A wave of panic crashed over Zoey, catching her in the undertow.

"Of course."

"I thought Dr. Parish wanted you to stay home and rest for a few days."

"And I did." Liz's rounded chin lifted a notch, as

if she were preparing for an argument. "Four days to be exact."

Zoey rubbed damp palms against her jeans. "Are you sure you wouldn't rather wait another week?" *Or two?* "Give yourself a little more time to get your strength back?"

"I'm sure." Liz rummaged through the top drawer of her dresser and pulled out a patterned silk scarf. "It's only an hour and I'll be sitting down. I miss Matthew's sermons and the fellowship."

Only an hour.

An hour surrounded by people who remembered the person Zoey had been, not the person she was becoming.

An hour of staring at Matt, who had begun to invade her thoughts *and* her dreams. But could never be a part of her future.

Chapter Eleven

"Mornin', Pastor." Daniel Redstone shuffled into the sanctuary. "You're here bright and early this morning."

Matt checked a smile. It didn't pay to point out the obvious—that Daniel had arrived at the church early, too. The elderly carpenter also served as the church's part-time custodian but refused to be paid for his work.

The men had become good friends, and when Matt needed an older man's advice, he often turned to Daniel.

"Just spending some time in prayer before the service." Matt prayed for everyone that walked through the doors on a Sunday morning. He didn't bother to mention that he'd been there since 6:00 a.m. Or that the majority of his conversation with the Lord had centered on Zoey.

Laughter danced in Daniel's coffee-brown eyes.

"I thought maybe you were taking Martha's place today."

Matt stared down at the piano keys. It probably did look a little odd, finding the pastor sitting at the piano instead of kneeling at the altar. "Are you kidding? I'm trying to draw people in, not send them running for cover with their hands over their ears."

Daniel chuckled. "The psalmist encouraged us to make a joyful noise, if you recall."

"And that's exactly what it would be. A joyful *noise*." Matt stood up and stretched, the dull ache in his back testifying to the length of time he'd been sitting on the wooden bench.

"I'll put a pot of coffee on." Daniel backed out of the sanctuary, the doors swishing shut behind him.

So Matt looked as dragged out as he felt.

Matt had spent a restless night thinking about Zoey. Remembering the way she had cuddled George as she shared a tiny piece of her past with him. Not content with that snippet, he had pushed for more. But just like last time, Zoey had shut down.

If his suspicions were correct, Zoey's parents had gone to Africa without her. Why? Had she wanted to stay in the States? Had their decision to leave Zoey with her grandparents triggered some sort of rebellion? If so, it didn't seem fair for people to hold something against her that must have happened when she was a teenager.

Isn't that why you never told anyone about Kristen? You were afraid you'd lose their respect.

The words burned a path through Matt's conscience. He hadn't told anyone about Kristen because it was part of his past. The part he'd put behind him when he had surrendered his life to Christ.

Nothing good could possibly come out of revisiting that particular time in his life.

It wasn't the same.

Zoey's fingers gripped the steering wheel.

She had dropped Gran off at the front door of the church and went to park the car. It was all she could do not to keep right on driving.

I don't think I can do this, Lord.

Two hours ago, just as Zoey suspected she would, her grandmother had come downstairs wearing the yellow blouse and a floral skirt. And then she cheerfully announced she felt well enough to go to the Sunday morning worship service.

That made one of them.

But Zoey had taken one look at Gran's face and knew she wasn't going to get out of it. She also knew she was going to feel the same way she had the first time she'd walked on stage.

The steeple bell began to chime and tears pricked Zoey's eyes.

You aren't alone.

The thought came unbidden, a warm promise smoothing out the edges of her panic.

Peeling her fingers off the steering wheel, she stumbled out of the car.

One foot in front of the other, she told herself. Just the way you've been doing it the past few months.

Except this felt more like a leap into a chasm.

"Zoey?"

Zoey's head snapped up.

Kate broke away from a group of people near the front doors and made her way over, her smile as vibrant as the auburn curls that escaped the loose knot at the base of her neck. "It's great to see you! I just talked to Liz. She's waiting for you inside. She always sits in the front pew on the left."

"If there's room in the front pew." Abby Porter suddenly appeared at Zoey's other side with a tall, dark-haired man in tow. "Zoey, this is my fiancé, Quinn O'Halloran." Abby leaned against him with a contented sigh."Quinn, this is Zoey Decker, Liz Decker's granddaughter—and the newest member of the Knit Our Hearts Together group."

Zoey might have argued the second point—except that the friends had taken up a collection on Friday evening. Zoey had become the proud recipient of a pair of knitting needles and, compliments of Emma Barlow, a skein of yarn in a shade of blue that happened to be Zoey's favorite color.

"Nice to meet you, Zoey."

"It's nice to meet you, too." Zoey couldn't help but feel a little tongue-tied as a pair of pewter-gray eyes met hers. Quinn O'Halloran had the same traffic-stopping good looks as Matt.

Abby had talked about her upcoming wedding the

night the knitting group had met. It sounded as if she wanted an intimate, outdoor ceremony at the bed and breakfast, but her older brother was pushing for a large affair in the ballroom of a swanky, family-owned hotel in Chicago.

With her fiancé—and the irrepressible Kate—in Abby's corner, it sounded as if she would get her way. But as she listened to Abby's dreams and plans, Zoey had found herself wishing that she could get to know her better and witness the couple exchange their vows.

And that, Zoey thought, was another reason she had to leave. Mirror Lake was part of her past, not her future.

"I better run downstairs and check the kitchen to make sure everything is set up for fellowship time after the service." Abby looped an arm around Zoey's shoulders and gave them a quick squeeze. "See you inside."

As the couple moved away, Kate rose up on her tiptoes, her gaze scanning the people gathered in the open foyer. "The service will be starting in a few minutes and I need to meet with the woman who volunteered to help me with a youth event tonight. Save me a spot?"

Zoey was so astonished by the request that it took her a moment to answer. "Sure."

"Great. I'll be back in a flash."

Zoey felt like a boat cut loose from its moorings when Kate darted away. She could feel the curious looks cast her way as she made her way down the hall to the sanctuary.

Fortunately, there was no sign of Matt.

So far, so good.

People's attention would be focused on Gran, and Zoey could keep a low profile.

Matt almost forgot to open the service in prayer when he looked out over the congregation and saw Zoey sitting next to Liz in the front pew. He hadn't expected to see Liz in church this morning either, considering the strict instructions Dr. Parish had given her not to venture out too quickly. House arrest, Liz had called it.

He tried to catch Zoey's eye, but her gaze remained riveted on the hymnal in her lap. She didn't even look up when Kate slid in beside her.

Matt had hoped that Zoey was beginning to relax a little, but her slender frame was as taut as a new bow. She looked as wary and tense as she had the day they'd met.

And she looked as if church was the last place she wanted to be.

Matt's heart sank.

Was it possible that Zoey wasn't a believer?

He wasn't naive enough to assume that being a preacher's kid guaranteed a commitment of faith, but he'd noticed the Bible Zoey had added to the box of clothing from the backseat of her car the day she arrived. And when something had upset her, she'd sought out the peace and solitude of the sanctuary, the way Matt often did when he was feeling discouraged.

Not only those things, but in the compassion and care she gave Liz, Matt saw the fruit of the spirit in Zoey's life.

There had to be another reason why she looked ready to bolt.

The choir led the people in the opening song, giving Matt an opportunity to collect his thoughts. When it ended, he stepped down from the altar until he was at eye-level view with the rest of the people.

"Good morning." Movement ceased and conversations dropped to a whisper. Matt smiled as everyone returned the greeting. "I'm glad you are here. If you are a guest this morning, we have a special gift for you. It's our way of saying thank you for joining us in worship."

Acknowledging visitors with a small gift had become an established tradition well before his arrival. The size of the congregation lent itself to what Matt had affectionately dubbed "family style" worship. It was one of the things he loved about Church of the Pines. Visitors never seemed to mind being singled out because most were relatives or friends of members of the congregation.

Matt glanced in Zoey's direction, waiting for Liz to stand up and introduce Zoey.

Only Liz wasn't there.

And the anguished look in Zoey's eyes momentarily stripped the air from Matt's lungs.

Following his gaze, people shifted in their seats.

If possible, Zoey's face lost even more color.

Mistake.

The thought ricocheted around his head as their eyes met.

A murmur rippled along the pews as Zoey slowly rose to her feet. She didn't say her name. She didn't say anything.

Trudy Kimball, who usually delighted in presenting the welcome baskets, had turned into a statue beside him.

Matt plucked the gift from her hands and made his way over to Zoey, who looked as if she were facing a firing squad.

"We're glad you could be here this morning." He stretched out his hand and felt Zoey's fingers, the tips as cold as if she had a case of frostbite, brush against his.

"Thank you." She wouldn't look at him.

Instead of asking her to introduce herself, Matt gave her hand a reassuring squeeze before he returned to the front.

She'd thanked him.

Now Matt hoped she would forgive him.

"Please join me in prayer."

Zoey closed her eyes, relieved the service had

finally come to a close as everyone's voices blended with Matt's husky baritone in the final "amen."

She had tried to lay her feelings before the Lord again—all her insecurities and doubts—but they began to creep in, almost as if they were lying in wait for her along the narrow aisle that stretched between her and the door. All she wanted to do was whisk Gran out the door...

"You're staying for fellowship hour, aren't you."

Zoey cringed. Kate Nichols seemed to have a gift for turning what would normally be a question into a statement of fact.

She'd forgotten about fellowship hour.

"I don't think..." Over Kate's shoulder, Zoey saw Rose Williams and several of her friends clustered by the door, staring at her with open disapproval.

"I heard Abby made the cinnamon rolls," Gran said with a wide smile. A smile that welcomed another opportunity to catch up with her friends.

"Great." Kate bounced to her feet as if the matter was settled.

"Great," Zoey echoed weakly.

"Liz Decker! Welcome back! We missed you around here." A woman with tufts of rooster-red hair reached over the pew and pulled Liz into a crushing embrace. "How was your stay in the hospital? Terrible! I knew it." The woman answered her own question while continuing to thump Liz on the back like she was a lump of bread dough.

"Do you remember Dr. McAllister's wife, Faye?" Kate murmured.

"Of course she remembers me," Faye bellowed. "I may be old, but there's nothing wrong with my hearing, Kate Nichols."

Kate snapped to attention like a soldier under inspection. "Of course not, ma'am."

Faye skewered Zoey with a look. "You're that Decker girl, aren't you?"

All Zoey could do was nod.

"Abby said she'd met you. I trust that young woman's judgment. Saw things in Quinn that no one else saw or wanted to see." Faye released Liz and stretched out her neck until she and Zoey were almost nose to nose. "I'm her bridesmaid, did she tell you that?"

"Wow." Zoey realized the proper response probably would have been "no."

"That's exactly what I said," Kate muttered.

"I heard that, too." Faye linked arms with Liz, who looked a little flushed. "Now, let's get downstairs before all of Abby's cinnamon rolls are gone."

Zoey had no choice but to follow.

As she trailed behind Kate, she saw Matt working his way through the crowd of people milling near the doors.

Zoey wanted to dive under a pew. Something told her that he was headed her way.

Rose Williams must have realized it, too, because her gaze bounced from Zoey to Matt and she frowned.

Reputation is very important.

The words had become branded in Zoey's mind. Rose's meaning had been clear, but it wasn't her reputation that Zoey was afraid would be called into question this time.

It was Matt's.

"Let's take a shortcut." Zoey cut through one of the empty rows.

"Hey!" Kate laughed. "Where's the fire?"

That's what Zoey was trying to prevent.

More damage.

Chapter Twelve

Kate knocked on the driver's side window and Zoey rolled it down, although she was more than ready to be on her way.

Fellowship hour had seemed to last a lifetime. As the minutes crawled by, Zoey managed to keep a watchful eye on Gran while dodging Matt's repeated attempts to talk to her.

Emma and Abby had brought their significant others over to the table Zoey had deliberately chosen in the corner of the fellowship hall, but their comforting presence hadn't been able to deflect the whispers and the pointed stares aimed in Zoey's direction.

Kate had disappeared for awhile, only to chase her down in the parking lot and delay her departure.

"I have a favor to ask." Kate crossed her arms in the window frame. "But you can always say no."

"No."

Kate ignored that. "The youth group is holding our

annual Bible Olympics tonight and I could really use an extra pair of hands. And eyes. I thought of you."

"Why?" Zoey asked bluntly. She couldn't wait to get away and now Kate was asking her to come back to the church—on purpose?

"Liz *might* have mentioned that you're involved with the youth at your home church. And she might have mentioned that you missed it." Kate didn't sound the least bit guilty.

Zoey's gaze swung to her grandmother. Liz returned her accusing look with a serene smile. Not a drop of guilt there either.

"It's from six to nine," Kate continued.

"I don't know if I should leave Gran that long," Zoey murmured.

"Delia is coming over this evening," Liz chimed in. "So yes, 'you can leave Gran that long.'"

Zoey was tempted to try and wiggle out of it, but she did miss the lively interaction with her "kids" in the senior high ministry. She had heard people claim that it took a special person to work with teenagers, but Zoey loved it.

She wasn't intimidated by their tough questions, nor afraid of their doubts. Zoey had come to discover that both were a natural part of the journey. In the Psalms, David had poured out his heart to God and it had brought them into a closer relationship. Over the past few months, Zoey had found that to be true.

Kate lowered her voice. "There will be chocolate. Lots of it."

"You don't have to bribe me."

"That wasn't a bribe, it was a statement of fact."

Either way, Zoey gave in. "I'll be there."

"Terrific. I'll swing by your place on my way to the church."

"You don't have to pick me up, Kate."

"Yes, I do. And I think you know why." Kate flashed her trademark smile. "See you at six."

After she'd gone, Zoey cast a sidelong glance at her grandmother. "Are you sure you don't mind me leaving for a while?"

Liz had tried to hide it, but Zoey had noticed that she'd seemed a little short of breath as they walked to the car.

"I don't expect you to stay with me every second of the day, sweetheart." Liz waved aside her concern. "You need to get out once in awhile, too. I'll be so busy trouncing Delia at Scrabble, I won't even know you're gone."

Zoey, who'd been "trounced" in the game several times over the past few days, smiled at the description. "All right."

Liz looked pleased. "You and Kate will get along fine. She's a wonderful girl. I don't think there's a person around here who isn't glad she decided to settle down in Mirror Lake. Most young people think small towns are dull."

At sixteen, Zoey had certainly thought so. She had never understood why her grandparents chose to retire to such an isolated part of the state. Until now. There was something special about Mirror Lake. Something in Zoey's soul that responded to the unspoiled beauty of the area and the unhurried pace of life. She only wished she had appreciated it sooner.

Matt stepped out of the church as Zoey put the car in gear.

Her gaze lingered on him for a moment. Today, in a charcoal-gray suit and a coordinating tie, he looked more like a pastor and less like the man in blue jeans who had tried to teach her Chopsticks. Unfortunately, her heart didn't seem to care.

Matt pivoted slowly, scanning the parking lot as if he were looking for someone.

Zoey stepped on the gas. But she couldn't prevent one last look in the rearview mirror.

Kate stood next to him. The redhead's expression was animated, one of her hands waving in the air like the conductor of a symphony as she talked. The other one rested on Matt's arm.

Were they a couple?

Zoey hadn't considered the possibility until now. They were close in age. Kate's lively temperament would mesh well with Matt's outgoing personality. And like Gran had pointed out, the woman had earned the respect of an entire community. People looked up to her. Admired her.

If Matt decided to marry, Kate would be exactly the kind of wife he needed.

The kind of wife he deserved.

* * *

That evening, Matt pushed open the front door of the church and found himself transported to ancient Greece. Paper torches filled with red cellophane "flames" lined his path through a backdrop of cardboard painted to look like stone ruins.

The Bible Olympics. Ordinarily the teenagers invited Matt to join in the games, but tonight he'd had to honor another commitment.

Neil, a forty-two-year old father of three had just found out he had cancer. Neil's wife had called Matt and asked if he would talk to her husband. She was a believer, but Neil thought that religion didn't get a person anywhere.

Matt had agreed. He'd used that as a launching point to tell Neil that it was a personal relationship with Christ that made all the difference.

The evening had started out with Neil being angry with God. It had ended with Neil being angry with Matt.

They were meeting again the next day.

Voices drew him down the narrow hallway. After collecting a devotional book from his office, he decided to stop in and thank Kate and the rest of the volunteers for their help. The small but dedicated team of youth leaders freed him up to spend more time on the mentoring ministry.

As he reached the sanctuary, Matt glanced down and saw that one of the doors had been propped open with a tennis shoe. Judging from the size, it had to belong to one of the Davis brothers.

He stooped down to pick it up and heard a chorus of muffled groans from inside.

"I don't like the songs we sing on Sunday morning. They're boring," one of the guys said.

"Boring, huh? Let's see what we can do about that."

Matt's feet melted to the floor when he recognized Zoey's voice. He pressed closer, trying to peer through the tangle of crepe paper vines and clusters of plastic grapes that decorated the narrow windows.

Zoey sat on the piano bench. In faded jeans and a long-sleeved T-shirt, her hair caught back in a colorful bandana, she could have passed for one of the teenagers gathered around her. "You remember the words to the praise song we learned tonight?"

Several heads bobbed up and down.

Matt couldn't quite make out what Zoey said next, but the short silence that followed didn't bode well for whatever she had suggested.

"All right." Zach Davis, the unofficial spokesman of the youth group, finally spoke up. "We'll try it."

Just as Matt was debating whether or not to make his presence known, Zoey unwittingly made up his mind.

She began to sing "Amazing Grace."

When Zoey reached the end of the first stanza, there was a brief hesitation and then some of the girls joined in with the chorus of a familiar worship song, encouraged by the competent sweep of Zoey's fingers against the worn ivory keys.

Matt sagged against the wall.

Zoey played the piano. And she played it *well*.

While he tried to wrap his mind around that, another thought jumped in.

What Zoey was doing shouldn't have worked. The blending of two totally different songs. One an old but beloved hymn, the other a more contemporary praise chorus. Somehow, though, she'd connected the two and created something new. Something beautiful.

Zoey, who had turned into an ice sculpture in church that morning when she thought she would have to stand up in front of the congregation and say her name, didn't appear the least bit self-conscious or hesitant now.

But that wasn't the reason he couldn't take his eyes off her.

If Matt had questioned whether or not she had a close relationship with God, he saw the answer in her face now.

This wasn't an experiment, a way to entertain a group of restless teenagers until their parents came to pick them up.

It was a reflection of something real. A song that wasn't printed on a piece of paper, but one that had its origin in Zoey's heart.

Matt had a feeling it was that, more than the music she had chosen, which encouraged their participation. How could a person *not* want to be a part of something so amazing?

The second time through, the teens' confidence had swelled, encouraged by the music flooding the sanctuary. Shoulder to shoulder, the girls swayed in time with the beat. And the boys—the self-conscious teenage boys that usually spoke in a series of grunts—were clapping their hands.

Until Tim Davis spotted him.

"Hey, Pastor Matt."

The music stopped abruptly and everyone turned to stare. Including Zoey.

"Hi, guys." Matt pushed his hands into the front pockets of his jeans and wandered in. "Where's Kate?"

"She's cleaning up the kitchen," Morgan Peterson said.

"Zoey was teaching us a new song."

"I heard." He tried to catch Zoey's eye, but her gaze remained fixed on the ivory keys now.

"Should I bring my guitar next week, Zoey?" The question came from Tim.

"You'll have to ask Kate," Zoey murmured.

Matt noticed the rigid set of her shoulders and knew he had ruined the moment.

"Ask Kate what?" Kate walked in, tugging at a wreath of plastic ivy perched on top of her head.

"If Zoey can help next week."

"I'll think of something else to bribe her with," Kate deadpanned. "Okay, everyone. I promised your parents we would be done by nine. You don't want me to get into trouble." She grinned. "Again."

Reluctantly, the kids gathered up their things, said their goodbyes and trooped out.

"What I heard sounded great, Zoey." Kate swooped down to retrieve a piece of green crepe paper stuck to the bottom of her leather sandal.

"Thanks," Zoey murmured.

"I didn't realize you were going to be here tonight." Matt was sure that after his colossal mistake this morning, Zoey would never show her face in church again.

Zoey didn't answer.

Kate's gaze bounced back and forth between them a few times. "Rachel couldn't be here tonight so I convinced Zoey to take her place. I gave her a choice between leading worship time or kitchen duty." Kate stifled a yawn. "I better take my own advice and head home. I have to be back at the cafe by 5:00 a.m. to make the pies."

"I'm sorry I had to miss the Olympics tonight. You did a great job pulling things together," Matt told her.

"I couldn't have done it without Zoey. The kids loved her." Kate shrugged her coat on. "Are you ready to go?"

"I can give Zoey a ride home," Matt offered.

Two pairs of eyes swung in his direction.

Kate struggled against a smile. And lost. "Really? Are you sure it's no trouble?"

"We do share a yard. It makes sense." Was it Matt's imagination, or did he sound a wee bit defensive?

"Oh, you're right. It makes *perfect* sense." Kate looked at Zoey. "Stop by the cafe tomorrow, okay? There will be a caramel apple pie with your name on it."

"That's not necessary," Zoey protested. "I enjoyed working with the youth."

"Did you hear that, Pastor? She *enjoyed* working with the youth. I want to clone her." Kate hoisted a purse the size of a small suitcase over her shoulder. "I could use your help again next Sunday night, Zoey. Think about it."

"I will." Zoey wore the slightly dazed expression of everyone who came into direct contact with Kate.

"Great. See you next time!" The hem of Kate's white robe fluttered like the wings of a tiny shorebird as she rushed from the room.

Leaving them alone.

"You know how stupid I feel right now, don't you?"

The softly spoken words fused Zoey to the piano bench. What she really wanted to do was disappear through the floor. She should have known Matt would see through Kate's not-so-subtle attempt at match-making. "I know. I'm sorry—"

"Chopsticks." Matt slid in beside her.

"W-what?"

He shifted his position and the movement

brought them even closer. Close enough for Zoey to see flecks of gold mixed in the green and brown palette of his eyes. "I tried to teach Mozart how to play Chopsticks."

Zoey's cheeks turned pink. "I'm no Mozart."

Matt's eyebrow lifted. "Care to tell me why you kept this talent a secret?"

Zoey peeked at him from under her lashes. "You asked me if could play like you did and I said no…"

Matt threw back his head and laughed. "Because there's no way you could mangle Chopsticks like I did. You told the truth. I get it."

Zoey's heart got tangled up in his laughter. All Matt had to do was enter the room and it seemed to get brighter. But they were here alone. Anyone could walk in and find them…Zoey refused to be the one to cast a shadow on his reputation.

"What I heard was incredible, Zoey." Matt stared down at her. "And the song you played for the youth group…where did you hear that? I've never heard anything like it."

"That's probably because I made it up," Zoey inched away from him and bailed off the other side of the bench. "I really should get home. Delia is keeping Gran company tonight, but she wanted to be home by nine."

She tried to scoot ahead, but Matt managed to catch up to her. He opened the passenger door of the truck and Zoey felt the soft press of his hand against the small of her back as she vaulted into the cab.

The door closed and Zoey stared out the window, grateful Matt couldn't see the effect he had on her. The slightest touch created a shower of sparks that lit up every nerve ending in her body like a Fourth of July sparkler.

She hadn't expected him to show up at the church. Kate had mentioned that Matt usually participated in special events, but that evening something had come up.

Knowing he wouldn't be there had taken some of the pressure off. Until Zoey had seen him standing in the doorway, staring at her as if he'd never seen her before.

"You know," Matt said slowly as he pulled out of the parking lot. "I've been rethinking the whole 'embarrass the visitors' part of the worship service."

It was the last thing Zoey expected him to say. Warmth bloomed inside of her. "Really?"

"Uh-huh. We can still give out a special welcome gift—after the service. What do you think?"

Zoey tipped her head to one side. "I like it."

"I hoped you would."

Zoey felt a smile coming on but was powerless to prevent it.

Matt realized that he waited for one of Zoey's smiles like a kid waited for Christmas day.

He guided the truck down the driveway and pulled over between the two houses. As Zoey opened the door, the light reflected off a shiny object on the seat.

"Wait a second. You forgot your Bible Olympics medal."

"I didn't forget it." Zoey winced as if she were in pain.

That could only mean one thing.

"What event did you win?"

"I can't remember."

"Uh-huh. Did the event you can't remember happen to involve a relay with gummy bears and a straw?"

"How did you know?"

"I won it last year."

"You didn't."

"Yes, I did. And I still can't look a gummy bear in the eye. Now hold still." Matt leaned forward and dropped the satin ribbon over her head. "And remember, the kids only make you compete in the humiliating events if they like you…" He flicked back a stray curl that got in the way.

Zoey stilled and Matt suddenly realized he was too close. Close enough to fall into those pearl-gray eyes and get lost.

"Zoey—" He wasn't sure what he'd been about to say but whatever it was, he didn't get a chance to say it.

The door closed with a snap and she was gone.

Chapter Thirteen

Zoey made a beeline for the house.

Why did Matt insist on being so nice to her? Didn't he know that every smile, every casual touch, turned into a fragile thread that linked them together? Made her want to stay?

Her hands shook as she peeled her coat off and hung it on the oak coat stand near the door. It was almost nine o'clock, which meant that Delia's son would be picking her up soon.

Zoey sucked in her lower lip, considering her options.

She wasn't sure she could face her grandmother and Delia yet. Gran would take one look at her flushed cheeks and know something was wrong.

George waddled up and pushed between her ankles.

"Miss me?" Zoey bent down and scratched the cat's patchwork velvet ears. George began to purr, which Zoey took as a "yes."

"You look thirsty," she whispered. "I'll bet you'd like some fresh water, wouldn't you? Maybe a bedtime snack?"

George's tail twitched.

That was good enough for Zoey.

George performed several graceful figure eights around Zoey's feet as she made her way to the kitchen. Through the window over the sink, she caught a glimpse of a familiar silhouette backlit behind the curtains in the carriage house.

Stop. Thinking. About. Him.

But how could she? Especially when she'd been thinking, no dreaming, about someone like Matt for years. Strong. Funny. Compassionate. A smile that melted her heart. Hazel eyes that promised to keep her secrets safe...

Until Matt found out what those secrets were.

Zoey tore her gaze away from the window and set George's ceramic bowl on the floor. "Here's what we're going to do. You're going to come with me to the parlor and be the adorable feline diversion. Do something cute so Gran and Delia won't ask questions."

Like who had brought her home? And why was she blushing?

George strolled over to the bowl, sniffed it once and strolled away again.

"Ready? Let's go."

George sat down and studiously began to lick one of her front paws.

"Fine. But I'm going to remember this when you bring me your catnip mouse tomorrow and want to play." Zoey glanced at her reflection in the toaster and tweaked a few rogue curls back in place. The curls Matt had disturbed when he'd placed the gold medal ribbon over her head.

Zoey groaned as she walked down the hall to the parlor. Better to face Gran and Delia than the memory of the brush of Matt's fingers against her hair.

She didn't *want* any memories of Matt. Nothing that would keep her awake at night. Nothing guaranteed to stir up dreams she had no business dreaming.

"I'm back—"

Zoey felt the room tip sideways.

Liz lay sprawled on the floor in front of the sofa, surrounded by a puddle of water and the splintered remains of a pitcher.

Zoey sank to the floor beside her grandmother, oblivious to the crunch of glass beneath her knees. Spots danced in front of her eyes as she gently lifted Liz's hand and checked for a pulse. Faint but steady.

"Gran?" She somehow managed to push the word out through lips that had gone as dry as chalk dust.

Liz moaned and her eyelids fluttered open. "Zoey? Are you all right?"

A bubble of hysterical laughter rose in Zoey's throat. "I'm fine. I think it's you we need to be worried about." She slid an arm underneath her grandmother's shoulders and helped her sit up.

Liz's eyes darkened with confusion. "I must have fallen asleep."

On the floor?

Zoey swallowed. "I think you fell, Gran."

"I couldn't have." Liz pressed a hand to her forehead. "I was watching television."

Zoey shifted and felt a slight sting in the bottom of her foot. Wincing, she plucked out a crescent-shaped piece of glass from her sock. "I'm going to call an ambulance."

"No." Liz clutched her arm. "That isn't necessary, sweetheart. I'll be fine."

She didn't *look* fine, Zoey thought as she helped her grandmother to her feet and guided her around the shards of glass to the sofa.

Liz sank limply against the cushion. "All I need is a glass of water."

"I'll be right back." Zoey backed out of the room. But instead of going to the kitchen, she slipped out the back door and sprinted across the yard.

Matt found himself staring out the window. Again.

Great.

If Zoey saw him, she'd think he was turning into some kind of stalker.

If she didn't think that already.

What was the matter with him?

He was so careful to maintain boundaries with women. He didn't even hug them. As a single pastor,

Matt never wanted to give someone the wrong idea or lead her on. He made an effort to keep his personal space...personal.

But that hadn't stopped him from trespassing into Zoey's.

I blew it, Lord.

A frantic pounding at the front door jerked him back to reality. Matt vaulted to his feet and braced himself for whatever emergency waited on the other side. If a crisis happened in Mirror Lake, the police took the first call, but it wasn't unusual at all for him to receive the second.

The last person Matt expected to see on the doorstep was Zoey, her eyes dark with panic.

"Hey." He reached for her instinctively, his hands closing around her arms. For a split second, she sagged against him and Matt's body absorbed the tremor that shook her slender frame from head to toe. "What's wrong?"

"Gran." Zoey gasped the word. "Can you come?"

Without a word, Matt pulled the door shut behind him and grabbed Zoey's hand, retracing her steps through the moonlit backyard. "Tell me what happened."

"She was lying on the floor when I got home." Zoey's breath came out in ragged pants between each word. "Delia was supposed to be with her but Gran was alone. I don't know how long. She doesn't remember falling but there's glass everywhere."

"Glass?"

"She must have dropped the water pitcher."

"Is she unconscious? Did you call 911?"

Zoey stumbled and Matt tightened his grip. "She told me not to. I shouldn't have listened to her, but I didn't know what else to do. She's lying on the sofa right now. She asked for a glass of water, but I came to get you instead."

"You did the right thing. The way Liz feels about hospitals at the moment, it might take both of us to convince her that she needs to take a trip to the ER." Matt gave Zoey's ice-cold fingers a reassuring squeeze as they reached the house.

"Matthew. What are you doing here?" Liz struggled to sit up straighter when they entered the parlor.

"Zoey is worried about you." He could see why. The only color in her face was a crimson stripe where her forehead must have connected with the floor.

"I'm as right as rain," Liz said. "I only wish I could say the same thing about my favorite pitcher."

Matt saw through her attempt to lighten the moment in an instant. Picking his way around the fragments of shattered glass, he sat down beside her on the sofa while Zoey hovered close by.

"What happened?" He lifted her wrist to take her pulse.

"Oh, it was my fault." Liz attempted a smile. "I tried to pour myself a glass of water, but I didn't think the pitcher would be that heavy. It slipped out of my hand and broke."

"Gran," Zoey interjected softly. "You were lying on the *floor* when I came in."

"I was trying to clean up the mess."

The uncertainty in Liz's voice worried him. "Are you feeling dizzy? Short of breath?"

Liz hesitated. "No."

He and Zoey exchanged a skeptical look over the older woman's head.

"Maybe we should take you to the—" Matt didn't get a chance to finish the sentence.

"*No.*" Liz's voice strengthened. "I must have over-done it a little today, that's all. I'll go up to bed now and I'm sure I'll feel better in the morning."

Matt glanced at Zoey. Her arms were folded over her chest, her eyes swirling with emotion.

"All right." He took hold of Liz's arm and drew her gently to her feet.

Zoey stepped forward to help but Liz clung to him. "No offense, sweetheart, but you wouldn't deprive me of the opportunity to lean on the shoulder of a handsome young man during my hike up the stairs, would you?"

A shadow of a smile touched the corner of Zoey's lips. "Of course not."

Matt grinned.

Liz's ability to find the humor in a difficult situation was one of the things he admired most about her. "That's a good idea. And while we're doing that, Zoey can call Dr. Parish and make sure he agrees with your plan."

"But—"

"No 'buts,' Gran," Zoey interrupted. "You might feel fine, but *I* would feel better if I talked to him."

Liz must have heard the wobble in Zoey's voice because she gave in. "All right."

"I'm sorry for causing such a fuss," Liz whispered as they moved toward the stairs. "All I remember is reaching for the water pitcher. The next thing I knew, Zoey was there. I didn't mean to scare her."

She'd scared them both. Matt wondered how much time had passed after Liz had fallen and before Zoey discovered her lying on the floor. "Zoey mentioned that Delia was supposed to come over tonight."

Liz had the grace to look guilty. "Her hip was bothering her. I told her to stay home, but I didn't tell Zoey because I knew she would cancel her plans with Kate." She glanced over her shoulder and her voice dropped to a whisper. "I'm worried that Zoey is going to blame herself for this."

"Why would she do that? She didn't know you were going to be alone. Or that you were going to fall," Matt pointed out.

"I know that and you know that, but Zoey…" Liz hesitated as they reached the top of the stairs. "She has a sensitive heart. She blames herself for a lot of things."

Matt remembered Zoey's expression when he opened the door and found her standing there. Worry mingled with a darker emotion.

Guilt?

"Will you talk to her? Find out what she's thinking?"

Matt nodded, knowing the first one would be easier than the second.

The relief on Liz's face brought some color back into her cheeks. Matt flipped on the light in her bedroom and guided her to a comfortable chair in the corner. "I'll send Zoey up to help you get settled."

Liz squeezed his arm. "Thank you."

Zoey was sweeping up the remainder of the glass in the parlor when Matt went back downstairs. His eyes narrowed on her stocking feet. "Are you limping?"

"I stepped on a piece of glass."

"Let me see."

"No!" Zoey held the broom in front of her like a shield. "I pulled it out. It's fine."

"Now you sound like Liz." Matt's hand cupped her elbow and he propelled her over to the chair by the fireplace. Ignoring her protests, he lifted the foot he'd noticed her favoring and peeled off a bright-green sock. "Stop squirming."

"I'm not squirm—ouch!" Zoey's breath hissed between her teeth as Matt's thumb found a sensitive spot on her heel.

"Sorry. I want to make sure there's no glass embedded under the skin." Zoey's pink-tipped toes curled under while he gently poked and prodded the perimeter around the cut. "What did Dr. Parish say?"

"I told him what happened and he didn't think

it sounded serious enough to warrant a trip to the emergency room. He does want to see her right away tomorrow morning." Zoey shifted in the chair. "He asked what she did today and agreed that she probably overdid it."

"When I saw her at church this morning, she looked great."

"She said she felt great, too." Zoey averted her gaze. "But I knew it was too soon."

Matt sat back on his heels and studied her profile. Liz's prediction had been right. Zoey *did* blame herself. "This wasn't your fault."

"I should never have let Gran go to church this morning, but she missed her friends…and your sermons. I thought she seemed out of breath when we were walking to the parking lot, but I didn't ask her about it." The words tumbled out in a rush. "And if I would have called to check on her tonight, I would have known she was alone."

"Liz's health might be a little fragile at the moment, but she's a very independent woman. The last thing she wants is to be treated like the pneumonia affected her ability to make good decisions," Matt said slowly. "Believe me, if you hadn't been here the last few days, Liz would have been running errands and making meals for people who are in better health than she is. If anything, you *prevented* her from having a relapse." Matt couldn't tell if he was getting through to her. "God doesn't make mistakes, you know. He knew what He was doing when He brought you here."

* * *

Zoey wanted to believe him.

Oh, she believed that God didn't make mistakes. That He knew what He was doing. But it had been so long since Zoey had felt as if she were part of His plan. It took time to absorb the sweetness of that truth. To let it resonate through her head until her heart picked up the refrain.

To avoid looking at Matt, she wrestled her sock back on. "I better go upstairs and help her get ready for bed."

Matt reached out a hand to steady her as she rose to her feet, and Zoey flinched. Because once again, his touch left her feeling curiously *unsteady*.

His hand fell to the side. "I'll finish cleaning up the rest of the mess before I go home. You'll call if you need me?"

Zoey hesitated.

"Let me rephrase that." Matt gave her a lopsided smile, the one that never failed to send her pulse into a happy little dance. "You'll call if you need me." This time, it wasn't a question.

But Zoey didn't want to need him. It was safer that way.

Then why was he the first one you ran to?

She pushed the thought away as quickly as it surfaced.

"I know, it's your job." A part of Zoey wondered just who it was she was reminding of that fact. "Pastors are on call twenty-four hours a day."

Being available was the unwritten clause at the bottom of his contract. And even though Zoey had begun to realize that being a pastor wasn't a career as much as it was a natural outlet for the man Matt already was, it was the only thing Zoey could think of to yank her heart back in line.

Matt didn't take offense at the flip response. He picked up the broom and met her gaze. The warmth in his eyes took her breath away.

"So are friends."

Chapter Fourteen

"Aren't you hungry?" Zoey couldn't help but notice that Liz was separating her half of the chicken pot pie she'd made for lunch into neat little sections instead of eating it.

Liz looked up. "I'm sorry, sweetheart. What did you say?"

"You don't seem to be very hungry."

The tip of Gran's butter knife nudged a wayward carrot around the plate. "I suppose my appetite isn't back to what it used to be."

Gran's appetite had been fine—until today.

Zoey bit her lip, wondering if disappointment was responsible for the faraway look in her grandmother's eyes.

The doctor's appointment hadn't gone as well as they had hoped. Dr. Parish had frowned his way through the checkup and then suggested that Liz wait another month to resume her normal activities.

It was something neither one of them had been prepared to hear.

Gran assumed her recovery time would be hastened by prayer along with a hearty dose of sheer will.

And Zoey had planned on leaving.

As much as she wanted to stay with Gran, Zoey wasn't sure how much longer she could remain in Mirror Lake. Not after realizing that Matthew Wilde posed a significant risk to her peace of mind.

And her heart.

Matt hadn't stopped over that morning before leaving for work, but a bouquet of sunny yellow daffodils graced the kitchen table when they returned from the clinic. The color alone should have lifted a person's spirits, but Liz had barely acknowledged them.

That worried Zoey, too. Liz was one of the most optimistic, faith-filled people she knew. It was obvious that something else was troubling her grandmother. Something more than being told to curtail her activities a few more weeks.

"Dr. Parish promised that the more you rest, the better you'll feel and the faster you'll recover." Zoey pushed her chair back and began to clear the lunch dishes from the table.

"Resting." Gran shook her head. "It seems like I've been doing plenty of that lately."

Zoey put her hand on her grandmother's shoulder and gave it a comforting squeeze. "You are. But you can't rush things."

"Knock knock." Matt appeared in the doorway and

Zoey's heart jumped up and down like a pogo stick in response. "Am I interrupting?"

"Of course not, Matthew." Liz mustered the first real smile Zoey had seen on her face that day. "We were just finishing lunch. Are you hungry?"

"I had breakfast at the cafe this morning. That means I won't need to eat again until June." Matt bent down and his arms enveloped Liz in a brief hug. "So, how did your doctor's appointment go this morning?"

She didn't answer.

Matt glanced up at Zoey, who responded with an almost imperceptible shake of her head.

His smile faded a little. "What did he say?"

"Dr. Parish is being overly cautious," Liz muttered.

"Define 'overly cautious.'"

"I can't resume my normal activities for a few more weeks."

"Four," Zoey said under her breath.

Matt flipped a chair away from the table and straddled it.

"You can trust Dr. Parish, Liz. If he tells you to take it easy, he has a good reason."

Liz's eyebrows dove together over the bridge of her nose.

"I know, but it feels like someone tied my hands behind my back."

"That's why you have Zoey." Matt said the words

matter-of-factly, as if she were the solution to a problem.

Or an answer to prayer.

He'd said the same thing last night. And Zoey had cradled the thought in her heart, almost afraid to believe it was true.

"And I don't know what I would have done without her," Liz agreed. "But I can't ask her to put her life on hold for me. She's Cinderella."

"Ella Cinders."

She and Matt said it at the exact same time.

Zoey stared at him in amazement, as if she hadn't expected him to remember a tiny, seemingly insignificant detail she had shared with him the day they met.

Matt couldn't exactly confess that he remembered everything about her. Not without sending her running for cover.

"Well, whatever her name is, Zoey is the leading lady," Liz maintained stoutly. "They need her."

Matt wanted to argue that Liz did, too.

What he needed was time.

Time to discover if the spark that flared between him and Zoey every time they were together was the result of simple attraction or the beginning of something more.

If that wasn't proof of the change in his heart, Matt didn't know what was.

Matt wasn't proud of his past behavior. In college,

his fraternity brothers had jokingly flipped his name around. Wilde Matt. Living for the moment had become his personal MO. When he wanted something, he had gone after it.

Like Kristen.

Matt thought he'd struck gold when he found a girl who viewed relationships the same way he did.

The memory still pressed against his conscience like an ache from an old injury. Over the past few years, Matt had started to think their final confrontation had cauterized his heart, sealing the wound from further damage but rendering it numb in the process.

It had also driven Matt to his knees. He'd hated the person he had become. When he finally got up again, his whole perspective had changed. So had he. A year later, certain of the path he knew God wanted him to take, Matt had applied to seminary. After he was accepted, he focused on his studies with the same passion and determination he had once devoted to having a good time.

Unless a person counted a few casual conversations over coffee, he hadn't dated since seminary. Hadn't met a woman who occupied his thoughts during the day and made him think about tomorrow.

Until now.

"Dr. Parish said that last night's episode was my body reminding me to slow down," Liz went on. "Besides that, it's only a few weeks—" Matt thought for sure he heard Zoey say "a month" under her breath again. "—I have food in the freezer and a nosy neighbor to keep an eye on me."

Liz wasn't fooling him. It sounded as if she were trying to convince herself more than them.

"Gran." Zoey sighed, a mixture of tenderness and exasperation that told Matt she saw right through the elderly woman's valiant smile. "I've already decided that I'm going to call Scott this afternoon and see if we can work something out. I've worked for three years without a vacation. He owes me."

He couldn't have heard her right.

Matt stared at her until a blush stole across her cheeks and reminded Matt that he was staring.

Liz looked more disturbed by the news than relieved. "Look at all the trouble I'm causing. Zoey has to ask for more time off. And what about the Easter cantata? The last time I talked to Diana, she hinted that she won't take it on. I've been praying about this for days and I'm trying to be patient, but we're running out of time. The whole community looks forward to it. I don't want to cancel it this year."

"Maybe we won't have to." Matt knew he would get into big trouble for this, but how could he ignore the fact that an answer to Liz's prayers—and his own—might very well be standing beside him?

The older woman's expression changed from worried to hopeful. "Do you have someone in mind?"

His gaze slid to Zoey. "As a matter of fact, I do."

There was a heartbeat of silence and then the

curtain of cherry-cola curls swung back and forth, as if she already knew what Matt was going to say.

"Oh, no. Absolutely not."

Understanding dawned in Liz's eyes. She sat up straighter in the chair. "But Zoey, you play the piano. And you know how to arrange music."

"And she sings," Matt added, deflecting Zoey's scowl with a wide smile. "I have another idea, too." In for a penny, in for a pound, as his mother used to say.

"What is it?" Liz looked delighted, even though she hadn't heard it yet.

Zoey looked as if could cheerfully strangle him.

"We could involve the teenagers this year."

Liz clapped her hands together. "Matthew, that's a wonderful idea. When did you come up with it?"

"Last night." After he'd heard Zoey play and watched the way she had drawn the kids in. Got them excited about worship.

"I'll be Zoey's consultant," Liz said without hesitation. "From my chair, of course. Following Dr. Parish's orders to the letter."

The orders she hadn't wanted to follow until now.

Matt hoped that Zoey noticed how quickly Liz's mood had bounced back. He'd planned to talk to Zoey first about directing the cantata, but Liz's obvious discouragement over Dr. Parish's orders had forced his hand.

"That's a great idea."

Matt slanted another look at Zoey. The expression on her face said she didn't agree.

"What. Were. You. Thinking?"

Zoey waited until she was alone with Matt to speak her mind.

And it hadn't been easy. Not with him looking as smug as the proverbial cat that swallowed the canary.

"I'm thinking the Easter cantata will go on as scheduled," he said easily. "And that Liz will have something to keep her mind off another month of limited activity."

"I can't do it." Zoey wasn't a pacer by nature, but she took a restless lap around the sofa.

"But you said yourself that your boss might agree to extend your vacation if you explained the situation."

Was that the only glitch Matt saw in his plan? That she might be denied a few extra weeks off?

"It's not only that." Zoey wrapped her arms around her middle and looked away.

"Liz agreed it's a good idea," Matt said softly. "And it will give her something to do. Something to look forward to."

Zoey resisted the urge to stamp her foot. She knew it would be childish but Matt wasn't playing fair.

"But Gran…" Zoey stopped. How could she explain that her grandmother seemed to possess an endless capacity to love? And forgive?

Zoey hadn't missed the disbelieving looks on the

faces of the people in Matt's congregation the day before. The uncomfortable silence that had swept through the sanctuary when people recognized her.

Zoey had sat there, raw and exposed, under the pressing weight of their stares. Swept back in time to a place she hadn't ever wanted to go back to again. Matt had apologized for putting her on the spot. Now he was asking her to willingly walk up to the front of the church and put herself on display?

On Easter Sunday?

And not only in front of the people who regularly attended Church of the Pines, but the entire community.

"I'm not a member of your church. Don't I have to pass some kind of test? Write an essay about how I came to know the Lord?"

Matt's smile did nothing to calm her fears. "You'll be working with Liz and under my direct supervision."

Direct supervision.

Was knowing that their paths would cross on a more frequent basis supposed to make her feel better?

"I've never done anything like this before."

"There's a first time for everything. And you are running out of excuses."

Zoey had one more.

Her past.

But she couldn't bring herself to say the words that would extinguish the grateful hope she'd seen in her grandmother's eyes.

Matt had backed her into a corner.

"I have no doubt that you can do it, Zoey."

Well, she did. And more than one.

"Why? Because I'm the daughter of a preacher? Because I know how to play the piano, so I'm expected to jump in and save the day?"

Matt's expression clouded, as if the thought never occurred to him. "No, because I heard you sing last night and I was…blessed. God gave you a gift. All I'm asking is that you consider sharing it."

A gift.

Zoey stared at him as those two simple words pierced her to the core. Accompanied by a reminder of something she'd been praying about the past few months.

Although she volunteered with the youth group, she hadn't joined the worship team at the church she attended. As much as she loved music, Zoey was still plagued by old criticisms and doubt. She was afraid to put herself out there again. Afraid that her gift would be rejected. The way she had been rejected.

"You're a different person than you used to be, Zoey," her friend, Melissa, had told her. "You have a new song. Don't be afraid to sing it."

But she was. So she'd been asking God to help her overcome that particular fear.

She'd just never imagined that Mirror Lake would be the place He would answer it.

"Okay." Zoey's voice didn't sound quite like her own. "I'll do it."

Matt stared at her, as if he couldn't believe she'd agreed.

Neither could she.

"Thank you."

If Matt had said anything else, Zoey might have changed her mind. He must have been afraid of that possibility, too, because he gave George's ears an affectionate ruffle and put his coat on.

He paused when he reached the door. "Zoey?"

Now what?

Zoey reluctantly met his gaze.

"As far as a test goes, there isn't one," he said. "And you don't have to worry about writing an essay about how you came to faith either." Amusement lit up the flecks of gold in Matt's eyes. "You told me that last night."

The door closed behind him and Zoey deflated into the nearest chair.

Last night?

She hadn't told him anything.

All she'd done was sing "Amazing Grace."

Chapter Fifteen

The center aisle of the church divided the choir members from the teenagers like a corridor through the Red Sea. Most of the kids sprawled on the floor around the piano had "grown up" in the church, but given the wary looks shooting back and forth between the two groups, one would think they had never laid eyes on each other before.

Zoey didn't know if she should be relieved or disgruntled that Matt wasn't among them.

She clamped down on a ragged breath, sent up a prayer for strength and tacked a smile on her face.

"Hello, everyone."

All eyes turned in her direction and a few half-hearted greetings stirred the air in both camps. Liz had said there were twelve people in the choir. A quick count told Zoey only half were in attendance tonight. The teenagers numbered eight.

Okay, Lord. Here we go.

"For those of you who don't know me, I'm Zoey

Decker." She stumbled forward, feeling like a puppet that was missing some strings. The binder began a slow descent through her moist palms.

Zoey hadn't had a case of stage fright like this since her first audition. And she wasn't even on stage.

"I'm sure Pastor Wilde has already told you that my grandmother, Liz Decker, isn't able to direct the Easter cantata this year due to some health issues. He asked me to fill in for her."

Silence.

Zoey found that slightly more encouraging than a mass stampede toward the door.

She licked her dry lips. "Let's take a few minutes to pray. That's the best way to start." Before bowing her head, Zoey saw a few of the teenage boys glance at the door.

It was possible she could lose one or two while her eyes were closed!

"Lord God, thank You for bringing us together tonight. This isn't about us—it's about You. We want to remember Your resurrection and celebrate the new life You gave each one of us." Zoey felt the prayer unfurl inside her, loosening the knot of anxiety and allowing peace to flood in and take its place.

An expectant hush followed her quiet amen.

"Liz explained the way the cantata has been done in the past, but—" That was as far as she got.

"Then she must have told you that Delia always starts with 'The Old Rugged Cross,'" Trudy Kimball interrupted.

A groan erupted from the teenage side.

Reminding Zoey there shouldn't *be* sides. "Everyone, please, take a seat for a few minutes. Get comfortable."

Just as she suspected they would, the choir filed obediently over to the front pew. The teenagers flopped down on the carpeted stairs.

Zoey's gaze swept over the group. Their expressions revealed everything from hopeful anticipation to outright skepticism. "The cantata doesn't have to look exactly the way it did last year," she said carefully. "We can change things if we want to. I'm open to new ideas and suggestions."

"Change things?" Delia's nose lifted as if she'd caught a whiff of something sour in the air.

"That's right." Zoey had spent a lot of time in prayer about the cantata and the message she hoped they could share. "You all know that a cantata is a collection of readings and songs, but it is even more than that. We can use the music to lead the people through the Easter story, to encourage them to think about the sacrifice Jesus made for us on the cross, not simply provide something to hum along with."

Several people looked confused, but Zoey saw other heads nod in agreement.

"I'll take down everyone's names and find out who prefers to sing and who would like to play an instrument." In the interest of keeping the peace—or rather, keeping it *peaceful*—Zoey decided to start with the teenagers. Some she recognized as members of the youth group, but there were a few new faces, too.

"Brandon White." A lanky teenage boy spoke up first. "Bass guitar."

A snort of laughter, quickly suppressed, followed the announcement.

Zoey, who had been thinking more along the lines of instruments that included trumpets and violins, gave him what she hoped was an encouraging smile. "We'll see what we can do."

It took some time to catalog the names and preferences of the teenagers. The boys collapsed against each other like dominoes if someone cracked a joke, and the girls used any disruption, no matter how short, to surreptitiously text on their cell phones.

Zoey felt as if she were trying to corral a litter of eight-week-old puppies. Finally, she turned her attention to the older members of the newly formed choir. Pen poised, she started with Trudy Kimball.

"I play the flute."

"That was in high school," Delia grumbled.

The woman deflated like a punctured balloon, leaving Zoey to repair the damage. "I'm so glad to hear that, Trudy. I was hoping to find someone who played the flute."

"You won't think so when you hear her play it," Delia muttered. Her pink cane, which seemed to have its own identity but not necessarily its own opinion, hit the floor in agreement.

Zoey took down the rest of the names, jotted a few

notes and took a deep breath, knowing that mixing up the two groups was going to be the challenging part.

She looked at Zach Davis, the easygoing high school junior who'd stunned her with his smooth-as-maple-syrup baritone on Sunday evening. Certain that his freckled face and engaging grin would win converts, she motioned him to sit with the choir. He bounded over to the front pew without hesitation and landed between Delia and Trudy.

Zoey slid onto the piano bench and ruffled through the sheet music her grandmother had given her from last year's cantata. "Since a lot of you are new, I'll give you a chance to choose your music and work on it at home before our next practice. We can go through a few of the traditional songs tonight, though."

"I'll start." Delia rose from the pew like a tiny, white-crested wave and made her way over to the piano. "Who is going to accompany me?"

"I will." Zoey almost smiled at Delia's look of surprise as she turned to "The Old Rugged Cross" and began to play softly.

As Delia began to sing, a dark-haired girl named Morgan unexpectedly joined in with the praise chorus Zoey had taught them.

To her credit, the older woman didn't miss a beat. And she didn't seem to mind that her solo was hijacked and turned into a duet. When they finished, the last note of the piano was followed by a burst of spontaneous, enthusiastic applause.

Morgan, who'd been lost in the song, came to and blushed. "I'm sorry."

"Don't apologize." It was exactly the way Zoey had envisioned the cantata. Fresh. Inspiring. "We want the music to stir peoples' hearts and remind them what God did for us. The cross bridged the gap—it changed everything. Understanding and accepting how much He loves us changes us, too. Sometimes it doesn't happen all at once, I know that from experience." Zoey paused and saw several of the choir members glance at each other. "But He is faithful on the journey."

"Amen!" Trudy Kimball murmured.

Zoey smiled and turned to Delia. "Mrs. Peake, how do you feel about sharing your solo with Morgan?"

"I'd be delighted."

Delia's cane struck the floor in agreement. Only Delia wasn't the one holding it this time. She'd leaned it against the pew right before she'd started singing. Tim Davis was the one who'd picked it up.

Zoey thought she heard an audible gulp from one of the kids sitting on the floor beside the piano.

Tim returned the cane with a sheepish smile. And a charming but mischievous bow. Delia opened her mouth, but Zoey jumped in before she could speak.

"Okay, I think that's enough tonight. Start practicing at home and we'll meet here again tomorrow night at seven o'clock."

The boys practically somersaulted across the room

on their way to the door, while the girls drifted along behind them at a slower pace.

Zoey began to collect her things, a dozen ideas already beginning to percolate. She would ask Kate to find out if the teenagers who weren't involved in the cantata would be interested in painting a special backdrop for the front of the church...

"Ahem."

Zoey pasted a smile on her face before she turned around. At least Delia had waited until the room cleared before she confronted her. "What can I do for you, Mrs. Peake?"

"What you said this evening about God's love changing people..."

Oh, no. Was Delia going to call her a hypocrite? Take Zoey to task for having the audacity to allude to the changes that God had made in her own life?

"I'm glad He is patient with us through the journey, too."

Zoey's breath lodged in her throat.

"You probably noticed some of the choir members were missing tonight," Delia continued.

"Yes," Zoey managed to say.

"They'll be here tomorrow. I'll make sure of it. Good night, Miss Decker."

It was all Zoey could do to remain upright. "Good night, Mrs. Peake."

Delia was marching toward the door. Just before she reached it, she paused long enough to toss her cane into the air like a baton. As it came back down,

Delia caught it, gave it an impressive twirl and tucked it neatly under her arm. Then, she glanced over her shoulder and gave Zoey what could only be described as a mischievous wink.

Matt leaned back in his chair and watched another vehicle pull out of the church parking lot. The only one left was a rusty purple Jeep.

All week long, the choir had been meeting to practice for the cantata.

He glanced at his watch.

Was it a good sign or a bad one that the practices Zoey scheduled seemed to be stretching further into the evenings?

Maybe he should ask.

The sound of footsteps in the hallway launched Matt to his feet. Zoey had a smile on her face and a spring in her step when he poked his head out of the office.

"Hi."

Zoey stumbled, then righted herself. "I didn't realize you were still here."

"The mentoring team met tonight, and I stayed a little longer to work on my sermon." Matt motioned her into his office. "I thought maybe you'd planned an all-night campout instead of a practice."

Zoey sighed. "We have a lot of work to do, and Easter isn't that far away."

"How did it go?"

A smile flickered in those pearl-gray eyes. "We had a few wrinkles to iron out."

"Can you fill me in on the way home?"

Zoey hugged the binder against her chest. "Sure."

"Great." Matt released the breath he hadn't realized he'd been holding. "Do you mind driving? I left my truck at home."

On purpose, but Zoey didn't need to know that.

They had been careful around each other the past few days. He had met Zoey coming and going from practices and they saw each other when he stopped by Liz's house to say hello, but Matt couldn't scale the invisible wall between them.

There were times he and Zoey shared a smile. Laughed together. Comfortable moments that Matt wanted to linger over. But at some point, she would catch herself and pull away. Almost as if she were obeying an inner warning to keep her guard up.

Matt didn't understand why.

As if to prove his point, Zoey took a hesitant step into his office and stopped.

"I've got to grab a few books from my library— otherwise known as the storage closet." He tossed a grin over his shoulder.

The phone on his desk rang as he searched the titles. "Can you get that, Zoey?"

It rang again…

"Church of the Pines," he heard Zoey say. A pause. "Hello? This is Zoey Decker…yes, he's right here."

Zoey held out the phone when he emerged from the closet. "It's for you."

"Hello?" Matt frowned at the silence on the other end.

"We must have gotten cut off. Did they leave a name?"

"No." Zoey looked worried as he hung up the phone.

"If it was important, they'll call back," he assured her. "And most of the congregation knows my cell phone number if there's an emergency. Ready?"

She glanced at the phone one more time and nodded.

Matt held the front door for her. A light, freezing drizzle had started to fall over the past few hours and Zoey bent her head against the sting of the wind. "I thought it was spring."

"This is spring in northern Wisconsin." Matt took hold of her arm as they sprinted toward the Jeep. He opened the driver's side door before making his way around to the other side.

Zoey blotted beads of moisture off her cheeks with the sleeve of her jacket before starting the Jeep. It growled a few times in protest before settling into a rough, uneven purr that reminded Matt of George.

"Okay." He leaned back. "Tell me about the wrinkles."

"Haylie Owens and Rob Price." Zoey put the car into gear and cranked up the heat. "Have you met them?"

Matt searched his inner database. "Rob is one of Zach Davis's friends. I've seen him at church a few times."

"According to Kate, Zach has been trying to get Rob more involved in the youth group. He plays the drums and Zach convinced him to come tonight by claiming it was a jam session. Haylie came with him."

"Zach and Tim Davis remind me of the disciples, James and John. They reach out to a lot of the kids at the high school."

"I was surprised Haylie stayed."

"What makes you say that?"

Zoey frowned. "She kept to herself most of the evening. It was pretty obvious she didn't want to be there, but Rob asked me if he could participate in the cantata."

"Do you have a spot for him?"

"Uh, that would be another one of the wrinkles."

Matt's eyebrows shot up. "Drums?"

"If Rob plays a quiet, measured beat on the bass drum right before the choir sings about the resurrection, it could be very powerful."

He thought about it and realized she was right. "You're the director." And he trusted her judgment.

The Jeep bucked as Zoey's foot stomped on the gas pedal.

"Really? Because drums would be something new."

"That's funny," Matt mused. "Because I distinctly

remember David talking about praising God with a variety of musical instruments in the Psalms."

Zoey bit her lip. "I just don't want to…cause any trouble for you."

"For me?" Matt looked at her in astonishment. "Why would it?"

Instead of answering the question, Zoey suddenly leaned forward and pointed to a slight figure walking down the sidewalk ahead of them. "That looks like Haylie, the girl I was telling you about." She pulled over to the side of the curb and rolled the window down. "Haylie?"

The girl paused at the sound of Zoey's voice. Her face twisted into a grimace as a gust of wind almost knocked her off her high-heel boots. Zoey waved her over and Haylie reluctantly approached the vehicle.

Matt took one look at the teenager's face and knew that her puffy, red-rimmed eyes hadn't been triggered by the weather. Without missing a beat, Zoey hopped out of the car and opened the back door.

"Hop in. We'll give you a ride home." She bundled Haylie into the backseat before the girl could protest.

Matt turned up the heat and adjusted both vents until they pointed directly at their shivering passenger.

Zoey got back in and unearthed a travel-size package of tissues from the console. "Here, take a couple of these. The rain made my mascara run, too."

"Thanks." A soft but unmistakable sniffle followed

the word and a hand reached between the seats to take the package Zoey offered.

Matt couldn't help but be impressed by Zoey's sensitivity.

She didn't put undue pressure on Haylie by asking embarrassing questions or trying to distract her with idle chatter.

When he'd stopped by the Grapevine for breakfast on Monday morning, Kate had mentioned again how the teenagers had gravitated toward Zoey even though it was the first time she'd served as a volunteer. Now he knew why. She didn't try too hard or make demands, which only made her more approachable.

"Haylie, the guy riding shotgun is Pastor Wilde."

Taking his cue from Zoey, Matt twisted around in his seat and gave her an easy smile. "It's nice to meet you."

Haylie mumbled a response and huddled deeper into the shadows.

"Where do you live, Haylie?" Zoey checked for traffic and pulled back onto the street.

"Keep going until you get to Oak Street and then take a right onto Silver Birch. It's by The Pines."

Matt wasn't sure if Zoey was familiar with that area. "Do you remember where that is?"

She kept her eyes fixed on the road.

"I remember."

Chapter Sixteen

Zoey's fingers tightened around the steering wheel.

How could she forget?

The trio of towering white pine trees that bowed over a narrow strip of shoreline had become a familiar local landmark. Because of its isolated location, The Pines had been a popular spot for impromptu beach parties.

In the two years Zoey had lived in Mirror Lake, she'd only been invited to one.

She turned off Main Street onto Silver Birch Drive and Haylie stirred in the backseat. "It's at the end of the road. The white house on the left."

The Pines loomed ahead of them. In the dark, it looked as if the road ended at the base of the trees.

Did the one in the middle still bear a scar from the impact of Tyler's car?

Help me, God.

Zoey was surprised that Matt couldn't hear her bones rattling around inside of her body.

One of the front tires hit a pothole and the Jeep lurched. Zoey realized she must have made some kind of sound because Matt shot a questioning look in her direction.

"Okay?"

Not even close, Zoey thought.

Haylie's seatbelt retracted before the car came to a complete stop in the driveway. "Thanks for the ride."

"I'll see you at practice tomorrow?"

"Bye, Zoey." The girl pretended not to hear the question, which, Zoey thought, was an answer in itself.

As Haylie ran up the sidewalk, a motion light came on, briefly illuminating a person standing on the porch.

Zoey wasn't one hundred percent certain, but she thought it looked like Rob Price. But if it was Rob, why hadn't he given her a ride home instead of making her walk almost five blocks in the freezing rain?

Thinking about Haylie momentarily shifted her thoughts from the accident. Until she looked up and saw the tree in the middle, its branches shaking as if it were still feeling the impact of a car...

Her fingers convulsed around the stick shift, and Zoey felt Matt's hand close over hers.

"Are you going to tell me why you're upset?"

She tore her gaze away from the tree.

"I was thinking about Haylie." It was partly the truth. "The weather is terrible. I wish she would have told me that she needed a ride."

Matt didn't say anything, but Zoey could see he didn't believe her.

She eased her hand away from his, her fingers trembling as she fumbled to turn the key in the ignition.

If Matt had the ability to read her thoughts so easily, did he know that she was falling in love with him?

Matt glanced up when he heard a quiet tap on the door of his office. Ever since he'd arrived at the church that morning, his thoughts had been more centered on Zoey than the notes from the mentoring meeting he'd attended the night before.

He pushed the papers aside. "Come in."

Walt Jenkins, who served as one of the elders in the church, shuffled in. "Mornin', Pastor."

"Hey, Walt." Matt smiled. "Have a seat."

Walt walked over to the window instead, his gaze bouncing around the room as if he'd never seen the inside of Matt's office before.

The man's behavior struck Matt as odd. "Is everything all right?"

"That's the question I was hoping you could answer for me," Walt said cryptically.

"I afraid I don't follow."

"I got a call last night. Thought I better get your side of the story."

His side of the story?

"A call? From who?"

"The woman who called asked to remain anonymous." Walt's lips pursed, as if the word had left a sour taste in his mouth. "Seems she heard a rumor that you hired Zoey Decker to fill in as the church secretary when Cheryl goes on maternity leave."

"What?"

"You know decisions like that have to be approved, Matt," Walt said. "Rose Williams's niece already volunteered to take Cheryl's place and we were planning to vote on it at the next meeting."

"We're still going to vote on it." Matt raked a hand through his hair. "I have no idea where this *anonymous* person came up with that idea, but it's not true."

Walt released a sigh. "Someone told this person that Zoey answered the phone. In *your* office."

Someone told…Matt wasn't so naive that he denied the existence and efficiency of the local grapevine, but he had never found himself tangled up in it. Until now.

"That was after hours," he explained. "We were in my office and Zoey picked up the phone because I asked her to."

Matt saw the grim look on Walt's face and realized he'd just made it worse. "Zoey was here for the cantata practice. We happened to be leaving church at the same time. I didn't offer her a position as my secretary and she wouldn't accept it even if I had.

She's only here for a few weeks—until Liz gets a clean bill of health from Dr. Parish and the cantata is over."

Walt swept the ball cap off his head and studied the Wisconsin Badgers logo embroidered on the brim. "That's another thing, Pastor. The cantata. You asked Zoey Decker to take over as the director without consulting anyone first."

Matt stared at him, unable to believe what he was hearing. "I didn't think I had to."

Walt cleared his throat. "Some people are…questioning her involvement, that's all."

It was clear that Walt, one of the men who went fishing with him on a regular basis, was one of those people.

"What's this really about?" Matt struggled to keep his frustration in check.

The silence between them deepened.

"People are talking," Walt finally said.

"About the cantata?"

"The cantata—and about you and Zoey Decker. The two of you seem to be spending a lot of time together."

"We live next door to each other," Matt pointed out. "Her grandmother is a good friend of mine. And if someone has a problem, I wish that person would talk to me and check the facts before spreading rumors."

Walt's wind-burned cheeks deepened in color. "It's

just that you don't know Zoey Decker like the rest of us do," he muttered.

"You're right," Matt agreed. "I think I know her better."

Matt was late.

Zoey glanced at the clock and then walked over to the kitchen window and peered outside. There was no sign of his truck in the driveway. No lights on in the carriage house.

Matt had talked to Gran earlier that morning and promised to be there for pizza night.

The day had dragged along as Zoey counted the minutes. She needed to talk to him.

And that, she acknowledged ruefully, would no doubt come as a shock to Matt, given the way she'd resisted his last attempt to coax her into telling him what was on her mind.

Their paths had crossed only a few times since the night they'd taken Haylie home. Zoey alternated her time between practices at the church and making sure that Gran wasn't overdoing things at home.

In between those responsibilities, she did her best to dodge Matt while trying to ignore the expanding hole in her chest when he wasn't around.

But she couldn't avoid him tonight.

She'd been encouraged when Haylie showed up for practice on Tuesday night and thrilled when the girl had shyly informed her that she played the violin.

Zoey had kept a watchful eye on Haylie throughout

the evening. In spite of all the commotion that came from assigning parts, listening to the selections and answering questions, she tried to stay in tune with the dynamics of the group.

It hadn't taken very long to figure out that Haylie didn't fit in. The rest of the girls, though polite, didn't go out of their way to include her. And some of the boys would nudge each other, glance Haylie's way and make comments under their breath. Zoey had assumed Haylie and Rob were dating, but at the last practice, he had all but ignored her. The girl had looked close to tears by the time practice ended but left before Zoey had an opportunity to talk to her.

And now she'd missed the last two practices.

Zoey had left a message on her cell phone several times, but Haylie hadn't returned her calls.

"No Matthew?" Liz shuffled into the kitchen.

"Not yet." Zoey's face heated at having been caught staring out the window. "It's been half an hour. Maybe we should start without him."

"I suppose so."

Neither of them moved.

"I'm surprised he didn't call to let us know that he couldn't make it," Zoey murmured, almost to herself.

"I think we should pray," Liz said briskly, taking Zoey's hand between her own.

Zoey closed her eyes.

"We don't know what's going on, Lord, but You do," Liz said quietly. "Whatever situation has kept

Matthew away tonight, we know he's not alone. You're with him. Whatever strength or encouragement he needs, we trust that you will provide it. Amen."

"Amen," Zoey echoed.

The next half hour crawled by. Gran asked questions about the cantata while they chopped up vegetables and prepared the crust, but Zoey recognized it as a means to distract her.

When the phone rang halfway through the meal, they both froze.

"That's probably Matthew now, calling to see if we saved him a slice of pizza." Liz was closer to the phone so she got to it first. "Hello?"

Zoey watched the color drain from her grandmother's face and her heart clenched. She pushed to her feet, her hands gripping the edge of the table for support.

"Yes, I'll call Delia and let her know. And please..." Liz's voice cracked. "Tell Matthew that we're praying."

Zoey was at her side in a moment. "What happened, Gran?"

Tears welled up in Liz's eyes. "Derek Cornell, one of the boys in Matthew's mentoring ministry, was playing with some friends by the lake this afternoon. They walked out onto the ice and Derek fell through."

"Oh, Gran, no," Zoey breathed. "Did he...is he all right?"

The night the knitting group came over, she

remembered Emma Barlow talking about the mentoring ministry that Church of the Pines had started the previous summer. Her son, Jeremy, had been matched up with Jake Sutton, which was how the couple had met.

"According to Cheryl, Matthew has been with Derek's mother for the past hour, waiting at the hospital for the Flight for Life helicopter to get there."

Zoey's heart sank even farther.

If the local hospital wasn't equipped to handle the situation, it could mean that Derek's condition was critical.

Her own legs were shaking, but Zoey managed to guide Liz back to the table. "Sit down for a minute, Gran."

"But I have to pass the message on to Delia," she said in a voice that wobbled. "She's next on the prayer chain."

"I'll call her." Zoey gave Liz a quick hug and sent up a fervent prayer of her own. For Derek and his mother.

And for Matt.

Chapter Seventeen

Backlit by the setting sun, The Pines didn't look as threatening as they had the night Zoey took Haylie home.

Zoey put the car in park and closed her eyes, struggling to replace the memory of shattered glass and twisted metal with the concerned look in Matt's eyes. The warm pressure of his hand closing around hers, offering her strength.

She wished he was with her now.

Zoey hadn't seen Matt since he'd driven to Milwaukee to sit with Derek's family. Over the past few days, it seemed as if the whole town was holding a collective breath, waiting for word about the boy's condition.

Zoey had been tempted to cancel practice for the cantata, but Liz and Delia talked her out of it. She had understood the wisdom behind their reasoning when she saw that shared concern over Derek's condition continued to strengthen the bond between the members of the newly formed choir. They prayed about the situation after every practice. The faith of the older women encouraged the teenagers to trust.

Haylie, however, hadn't been there to experience it.

Zoey got out of the vehicle and walked slowly up the sidewalk.

I know you're with me, Lord. Give me the right words to say to her.

The curtains on the bay window quivered as Zoey rang the doorbell. A few minutes later, a little boy about five years old with a hank of gold hair and eyes the same shade of blue as Haylie's opened the door.

"Hi." Zoey took a deep breath. "Is Haylie here?"

"Nope." The boy tucked his chin and offered a shy smile.

"My name is Zoey."

"Ben, close that door and get back in here…" The woman whose face was an older, careworn version of Haylie's pulled up short when she saw Zoey. Her eyes narrowed. "Who are you?"

Ben took advantage of the distraction and darted away.

"I'm Zoey Decker. Haylie and I have been working together on the Easter cantata at Church of the Pines," Zoey explained. "I just wanted to talk to her a few minutes."

"She took off about an hour ago."

"Do you know when she'll be back?"

Either Haylie's mother heard the note of desperation

that crept into Zoey's voice or she didn't want to deal with the possibility of a future visit, because she pointed down the road. "Sometimes she takes a walk down by The Pines. There's a rock she likes to sit on." The woman rolled her eyes. "Don't ask me why."

Zoey didn't have to. She had claimed her own places of solitude when she was seventeen.

"Thank you, Mrs. Owens."

"If you find Haylie, remind her that she has to take care of Ben tonight. I'm working third shift." The door closed with a decisive snap between them.

Zoey dipped a hand into her pocket, her fingers curling around her cell phone. She could call…

But Haylie wouldn't answer.

A breeze ruffled Zoey's hair as she pivoted toward the three trees that stood like sentinels on a narrow strip of land that followed the curve of the road.

She started walking, her steps slow, her heart racing.

Haylie was there, just as her mother had predicted. But she wasn't perched on one of the granite boulders scattered along the shoreline. She sat right at the foot of the three massive pine trees Zoey had been doing her best to avoid.

It was the girl's posture, arms hugging her chest, chin resting on her knees, that prevented Zoey from retreating to the safety of her Jeep.

She lowered herself onto the damp, spongy ground next to Haylie. "Hi."

"What do you want?"

Zoey tried not to take the girl's attitude personally.

"I missed you at practice yesterday."

Haylie shrugged.

"Will you be there tomorrow?"

"I don't think so." Haylie leaned back, hooked her thumbs through the loops on the waistband of her jeans and looked bored.

Zoey, who had perfected the "and-you-can't-make-me" pose when she was Haylie's age, wasn't intimidated. "Why not?"

"Maybe I don't want to."

Except that she did.

Zoey could see the battle going on in Haylie's eyes, a reflection of what was happening in her heart. Having fought on the same field, she recognized the signs.

"Did something happen?"

"I don't belong there, okay?" The words burst out of Haylie.

"There?"

"At church." Haylie snapped the words, as if Zoey should have known that's what she meant.

"Why would you say that?"

"Are you kidding me? The only reason I went there in the first place was because of Rob. We've been… hanging out for a couple of months and he kept talking about how cool it was. How much he liked it."

Zoey knew that Haylie was watching her closely—looking for signs of shock or disgust that she'd come to youth group because of a boy.

Haylie didn't know it yet, but she wasn't going to get rid of her that easily.

Under different circumstances, Zoey wouldn't have pushed. But where would she be now if Melissa hadn't obeyed that nudge from the Lord and asked her some tough questions?

"What made you change your mind?"

Haylie scraped at what remained of the bright-yellow nail polish on her thumb. "It doesn't make any sense."

Zoey waited.

"The songs. Those verses that you have Tim Davis read out of the Bible. All the stuff about Jesus dying on the cross for people's sins…" Haylie bit down on her lip to prevent the rest of the words from rushing out.

"You don't believe it?"

Haylie looked down at her feet and Zoey understood.

"He didn't just die on the cross for people's sins," Zoey said carefully. "He did it for me. And for you."

"Not for me," Haylie whispered. "I've messed up. You don't understand."

"Oh, I understand messing up." They were sitting in the shadow of one of Zoey's biggest mistakes.

A tear rolled down Haylie's cheek. "Me and Rob... we were together before he started to go to church with Zach. I really like him, but the rest of the guys have been giving him a hard time, saying things about me. Rob is confused and he won't even talk to me now. I guess after the things we did, I'm not...good enough to be there."

Zoey read between the lines, and her heart ached over the decisions Haylie had made that were tearing her apart.

Give me wisdom, Lord. Help me find the words.

For the first time since the accident, Zoey could look at the trees. Really look at them. A wide gash in the trunk of the middle one had scabbed over like a wound.

She reached out to touch a cluster of tiny green shoots protruding from the center of the mark, overwhelmed by the simple but humbling reminder of what God could do. Not only with a tree, but a person's life.

"We've all made mistakes, Haylie, every one of us," Zoey said. "God knows we're not perfect. But Jesus was. It says in the book of Romans that Christ died for us while we were still sinners. He doesn't wait until we have our act together. We don't have to clean ourselves up before we approach Him. We can't. That's where grace comes in. We need Him. And He loves us. He loves you. We can't undo the past. But with God's help, we can move forward."

"I don't know." The wide blue eyes held doubt—and a flicker of longing.

"I do," Zoey said, knowing it was time to tell her story. "Because He's helping me."

A combination of little sleep, hospital food and being there for Derek's mom through those first, crucial twenty-four hours had left Matt with a chilling numbness that had seeped through his body. And his spirit.

Late Thursday night he had stopped home long enough to throw a few things into his suitcase. It was a long drive to the Milwaukee Children's Hospital and knowing that Angela, Derek's mother, was waiting there alone for word on her son's condition, Matt hadn't wanted to waste a minute.

The call had come in a few minutes before Matt had left for the day. Three adolescent boys had been playing on a large chunk of ice that had broken away from the shoreline. Derek had slipped off the side and fallen in. By the time his friends managed to get to shore and call for help, he had disappeared below the surface of the frigid water.

Jake Sutton had put a call through to Matt while on his way to the scene.

He'd been there when Derek was pulled from the water.

Matt dragged a hand through his hair and cracked open the car window. Fresh air poured in and stung Matt's eyes. He almost welcomed the pain, hoping it would burn through the fog that had rolled over him.

Derek's condition had stabilized during the night, so Matt reluctantly made the decision to return to Mirror Lake. He had two dozen voicemail messages that he hadn't answered. A sermon to deliver the next day that he hadn't written yet. And prayers that started out strong but quickly wilted like plants exposed to frost.

Matt was disappointed with God.

He knew it. He knew that God knew it. But at the moment, *knowing* it didn't allow him to shed the feeling the way a person would an itchy sweater.

Angela had recently started to attend church. An abusive marriage had left her scarred, not only physically but emotionally, but the positive changes she'd seen in her son's life through the mentoring program had made her curious.

Matt could only pray that after what happened to Derek, his mother would turn to God for comfort rather than away from Him.

Liz's house came into view as he turned the corner. He owed both her and Zoey an apology for standing them up on Thursday night, even though he knew they would understand.

He hadn't even had time to call. The world had shrunk to the size of the ICU waiting room. It had reminded him of a medical no-man's-land, inhabited by strangers who had nothing in common except for the fact they'd been thrown together by a crisis.

Matt had done what he could, not only for Angela, but also for the handful of weary people camped out in the uncomfortable chairs and on the floor, all of them waiting for news, good or bad. Matt had handed out cold drinks. Distributed snacks from the vending machine. He'd even occupied a rambunctious two-year-old while his weary mother took a short nap.

Matt unlocked the door and dropped his duffel bag on the rug before collapsing in the recliner.

He should have been ready to sleep for a week, but while every muscle in his body screamed for rest, his mind refused to shut down.

He closed his eyes and tried to pray again, but the words continued to dance out of his reach.

A faint knock on the door roused him just as he started to doze off. Matt considered ignoring it. He had called Cheryl before leaving the hospital and asked her to put the latest news about Derek on the prayer chain. He hadn't told the secretary what time he planned to return to Mirror Lake, only that he would be back in time for the Sunday morning service.

Matt wasn't sure he was ready for visitors.

Stumbling toward the door, he opened it and found Zoey on the front step, George cradled in her arms.

"Hey…" Matt's brain felt as sluggish as if it were only firing on two cylinders.

"Hi." Zoey's gaze swept over him, and Matt knew exactly what she was seeing. A rumpled cotton shirt, wrinkled khakis and bare feet. "I saw your truck in the driveway."

"I just got back about an hour ago."

Zoey continued to study him. "I brought George over so you'd have someone to practice your sermon on."

The sermon he hadn't started writing.

Spots floated in front of his eyes, but Matt couldn't seem to blink them away. He was a little embarrassed that Zoey was seeing him like this.

Weak. Discouraged.

"I was trying to take a nap."

"No, you weren't."

"Look, Zoey." Matt released a sigh. "I don't mean to be rude, but I'm not really…up to company."

"I understand." Zoey transferred George into his arms and walked past him into the house.

Zoey held her breath, waiting for Matt to stop her.

Maybe she should have taken his not-so-subtle hint and left him alone. One look at his face, however, told her that although it might be what Matt wanted, it wasn't what he needed.

For the past two days, Zoey had been watching for his pickup truck. When she'd glanced outside and saw it parked in the driveway, her heart had tilted like an amusement park ride.

As far as she knew, Matt hadn't told anyone that he was back.

She had waited for him to drop in and say hello.

But he hadn't. He hadn't called either.

For the next half hour, Zoey tackled every chore that gave her a view of the house next door. Dusting windowsills. Dusting the knickknacks *on* the windowsills.

As the afternoon sun began to slip below the trees, she waited for the lights in the carriage house to come on.

Nothing.

Finally, Zoey hadn't been able to stand it any longer.

"Gran?"

Liz, who been channel surfing and stumbled upon her favorite musical, barely glanced in her direction. "Mmm?"

"I'm going out for a few minutes. If you need anything, call my cell phone, okay?"

Liz waved a tissue, which Zoey took as an affirmative.

Covering the distance between the two houses in record time, she'd rapped on Matt's door. The house was so dark that Zoey had started to wonder if he had walked over to the church.

Until she'd heard the slow, heavy tread of footsteps on the other side. The door opened and Zoey saw a stranger. A gray-faced, exhausted stranger.

It was obvious Matt hadn't slept much in the past forty-eight hours. But there was something else that concerned Zoey even more. He looked… discouraged.

Now that she was inside the house, Zoey wasn't sure quite what to do.

With hands that shook, she dumped out the remains of the coffee and rinsed it out before putting on a fresh pot. In the refrigerator, she found the ingredients to make a simple ham and cheese omelet and dug a skillet out of the cupboard.

When she finally scraped up the courage to glance over her shoulder, Matt sat slumped in a corner of the sofa, George curled up in his lap, as if arguing with her would have used up too much energy.

Good. She had no intention of leaving until she was sure that he was okay.

While the omelet cooked, Zoey collected the dirty dishes that Matt hadn't had time to deal with on Thursday, put them in the dishwasher and straightened up the kitchen.

When the meal was ready, she arranged everything on a tray and delivered it to the coffee table.

Neither of them said a word.

But Zoey talked to God while Matt devoured the omelet and toast as if he hadn't eaten for days. Maybe he hadn't.

What should I say, Lord? I can tell that he's hurting. I don't know what to do…

She had memorized so many scripture passages but none came to mind. Her heart ached with his.

Zoey kicked off her shoes and sat down beside him, tucking her feet underneath her. Matt still didn't speak. He didn't tell her what the past two days had been like. He didn't pretend that seeing an eleven-year-old boy so close to death hadn't changed him.

They sat like that for another hour until shadows stretched along the walls and both of Zoey's feet began to tingle.

When she thought Matt was asleep, she got up gingerly and flexed her muscles. Grabbing an afghan off the back of the sofa, she covered Matt up, whispered to George to be good and padded toward the front door.

"Zoey?"

She turned around. Matt was smiling at her. A tired, rusty kind of smile that went straight to her heart.

"Thanks for listening."

"But…you didn't say anything."

"That's what I mean. You heard everything I didn't say."

Zoey returned his smile with a tentative one of her own. "You're welcome."

Chapter Eighteen

The teenagers had cleared out after practice, but Matt heard music coming from the sanctuary. He leaned against the wall and listened for a few minutes before making his presence known.

Although Zoey planned to accompany some of the choir members on the piano, he hadn't heard her sing again until now.

He knew the exact moment that Zoey realized he was there. Her shoulders stiffened and she stopped playing.

"You are really gifted."

"I'm really out of practice," Zoey contradicted with a wry smile. "I haven't played this particular song for almost a month."

"It sounded great to me."

"Do you sing?"

"I've been likened to a truck idling," Matt admitted cheerfully.

That drew a smile. "I can leave if you're ready to lock up for the day."

"No rush." He wandered over and saw the script resting in the music stand by the piano. Matt picked it up and examined the cover. On top of a satin pillow sat a pink tennis shoe instead of a glass slipper. "'*Once Upon a Castle,*' right?"

"It opened last weekend. I thought I better run through the script a few times, or my understudy will take over my job completely."

Matt's heart felt as if it had hit a speed bump. He was all too aware of the fact that Zoey would be leaving the week after Easter.

Her unexpected visit to his house the day he'd come back from the hospital had been a gift. An indication that maybe, just maybe, she had some feelings for him, too.

The memory still blew him away. He was used to being the one people turned to in a crisis. The strong one. But somehow, Zoey had known exactly what to say to put things in perspective.

Nothing.

She had simply been there for him. She'd shared George with him. Fed him. Sat with him.

And all the while, Matt sensed she had been praying for him, too.

He wanted to ask Zoey out on a real date. Let her know how he felt about her. But Matt was also sensitive to the timing. He didn't want to rush Zoey. And he didn't want to rush ahead of God either.

"I won't bother you, then." He turned to go, but Zoey put her hand on his arm.

"Matt, wait a second. I have to talk to you about something."

The serious look on her face told Matt that he should sit down before he heard what it was. He lowered himself to the carpeted step and looked up at her expectantly.

"I talked to Haylie while you were gone," Zoey said. "She was planning to play the violin for the cantata, but then she skipped a few practices."

"Is everything okay?"

"It depends on what you mean by 'okay.'" Zoey sat down next to him. "She and Rob have been…spending a lot of time together over the past few months. I think they're both dealing with some heavy-duty guilt over their relationship."

Matt felt a sharp pain slide between his ribs. He knew all about that kind of guilt.

"I want to do the right thing, Kristen. We can get married. I'll take care of you and the baby."

Kristen had laughed at him.

"You don't have to take care of anyone, Matt. I didn't think you were so old fashioned. I'm not about to throw away my future because of one mistake. I just thought you'd want to know so you'd be more careful next time."

Up until that point, Matt hadn't thought about the consequences of his behavior. All he'd thought about was having a good time.

After informing him that she was pregnant, Kristen refused to talk to him again. When Matt no longer saw her on campus, he tracked down her former roommate and discovered that Kristen had dropped out of school at the end of the semester. When he pushed for more information, the girl had reluctantly told him that Kristen claimed to have suffered a miscarriage early in her first trimester.

But Matt had always wondered if it were true or if Kristen had terminated her pregnancy.

It was his roommate, the guy Matt had frequently scoffed at for his values, who had seen the guilt eating him alive and told him how to find peace.

"I'm glad Haylie talked to you."

"It wasn't easy for either of us," Zoey admitted. "But people need to know they're not alone in their pain. I think that's one of the ways God uses the mistakes we've made for good. To comfort others in the way we've been comforted, like it says in the Bible."

"Second Corinthians." Matt knew the verse Zoey was referring to but he—someone who studied the scriptures on a daily basis—hadn't thought about it in terms of his own life before now.

"Matt?" Zoey's voice barely registered through the rushing sound in his ears. "Will you talk to Rob?"

"Maybe he would probably be more comfortable talking with Cal," Matt heard himself say. "He's been leading a weekly Bible study for the high school boys."

Zoey couldn't quite hide her disappointment. In him. She rose to her feet. "I should practice a little more. Delia invited Gran over for supper tonight, so I have a little extra time."

"Zoey…" Matt stopped. How could he explain that his reluctance to talk to Rob about relationships stemmed from the mistakes he had made in that area? Mistakes that had not only affected him, but the young woman he'd been dating and the life of an unborn child he hadn't even bothered to consider at the time?

Matt normally didn't shy away from difficult situations. It wasn't easy to admit he'd been ready to avoid helping someone because it hit too close to a wound on his own soul.

"'Scuse me, Pastor." Daniel Redstone paused in the doorway, a smile lifting the corner of his lips when he spotted Zoey sitting at the piano. It was encouraging to know that not everyone questioned Matt's friendship with Zoey. "There's someone out here who wants to talk to you."

"I'll be right there." Matt stood up, hiding his frustration at the interruption. "If you stick around awhile, I'll help you practice your lines." And try to gather the courage to explain why he'd resisted her suggestion that he talk to Rob.

For a moment, he thought Zoey would reject his offer. Until she smiled. "I'm not going anywhere."

Matt wished he could hold her to that.

As he walked down the hall, he expected to see one

of the members of his congregation waiting for him. The woman examining the bulletin board on the wall outside his office only looked vaguely familiar.

Daniel veered off toward the Sunday school rooms, leaving Matt alone to work out the introductions. He found that a little strange, considering how friendly the carpenter was to everyone.

"Hello."

She jerked her head in lieu of a greeting. "Pastor Wilde Thank you for meeting with me on such short notice."

There had been *no* notice, but Matt didn't point that out.

"We can talk in my office, if you'd like."

Another short nod and she swept into the room ahead of him.

Matt gestured toward one of the comfortable chairs opposite his desk. "Please, have a seat, Mrs… "

"Galway. Gina Galway."

He knew he had seen the woman somewhere before, but everyone in a town the size of Mirror Lake was at least a familiar face, if not a name.

"I'm sorry to drop in like this." Gina Galway gathered her oversize purse in front of her like a shield. "I did try to call but no one answered the phone."

"I'm sorry. The secretary took the afternoon off. What can I do for you?"

"Normally, I wouldn't interfere, but Liz Decker is practically my neighbor and I wanted to be sure that someone is looking out for her best interests."

Galway.

Now he knew why she looked familiar. She lived down the block from Liz.

"Liz is doing great." Matt assumed she had heard about Liz's slight relapse the week before through the neighborhood grapevine.

"I don't know how she could be, with the added stress in her life," Gina murmured.

"I'm afraid I don't follow you." Matt frowned. "Added stress?"

"Her granddaughter. Zoey Decker."

The air emptied out of Matt's lungs. "Mrs. Galway…"

He didn't get an opportunity to finish.

"I would think that you of all people—the pastor Liz claims to respect so much—would have sent that young woman packing the day she arrived. But instead, I heard a rumor that you actually put her in charge of this year's Easter cantata." Gina paused to take a breath. "Please tell me that isn't true."

"She's more than qualified for the position. I've gotten to know Zoey over the past few weeks and I'm confident she will do a wonderful job."

"She's an *actress*." Gina said it with a sneer that made Matt's blood boil. "That means she gets paid to pretend to be someone she isn't. It's obvious she pulled the wool over your eyes, too."

"Mrs. Galway—"

"Zoey Decker was nothing but trouble when she lived with Liz and Jonathan," Gina interrupted.

"That was a long time ago," Matt said slowly. "I understand that Zoey was a teenager when she lived in Mirror Lake."

"Old enough to know right from wrong," Gina snapped. "Sneaking out of the house at all hours. Breaking the rules and lying about it. Liz and Jonathan tried to do the right thing. Took the girl in when her own parents couldn't handle her anymore, but everyone could see the toll it took on that poor couple. It was plain to see that Zoey never cared about anyone but herself."

Images of Zoey flashed through his mind. The look on her face the night Liz had fallen. The way she'd cuddled George in her lap. The compassion in her eyes when she'd told him about Haylie.

"It isn't uncommon for teenagers to rebel in some way." Matt struggled to keep his voice even. "Most of it is harmless."

Gina looked shocked that Matt would take up Zoey's defense.

"I don't consider causing someone's death a harmless act of rebellion, do you, Pastor Wilde?"

Matt felt the room tilt.

"What are you talking about?"

"Liz didn't tell you about Tyler Curtis?" Gina saw his confusion and shook her head. "I shouldn't be surprised. She insists on seeing the best in everyone, whether they deserve it or not. And after what she did, Zoey Decker definitely does *not* deserve it."

Matt couldn't listen to any more. He stood up and

walked to the door. "Thank you for stopping by, Mrs. Galway. Like I said, I've gotten to know Zoey and I promise that you have nothing to worry about."

The woman followed his lead and rose to her feet. "Maybe *you* should be worried, Pastor Wilde. Up until now, you've been a respected leader in the community. People trusted your judgment. From what I've heard, that isn't the case anymore." Gina's eyes narrowed. "People in the community usually attend the cantata, but if you insist on allowing Zoey Decker to be involved in it this year, things may not turn out quite the way you planned."

"I appreciate your concern," Matt said through gritted teeth.

"There might a lot of empty spaces in the pews on Easter morning." Gina spoke slowly, as if she were afraid Matt wasn't catching on.

"I'm sorry there are people in Mirror Lake who feel that way."

"That just proves how she's blinded you," Gina snapped. "It's not just people in the community who don't want to be reminded of what Zoey did. Some of those empty pews are going to be there because people in your own congregation feel the same way."

Matt opened the door and Gina brushed past him, the heels of her shoes clicking as she headed toward the door.

The hostility emanating from Gina Galway disturbed Matt more than the veiled threat. She really believed the things she had said about Zoey.

Out of the corner of his eye, he saw a movement further down the hall. Zoey stood in the shadows, her face drained of color.

In that instant, Matt realized she'd heard everything Gina Galway had said.

Zoey's feet refused to move.

She had received a call from Haylie on her cell phone, asking if Zoey could stop by the Grapevine Cafe for a few minutes to talk.

Haylie hadn't told her what it was about so Zoey hadn't wanted to refuse. She'd ventured down the hall, hoping to track down Daniel and ask him to pass a message on to Matt.

There'd been no sign of Daniel, but the door to Matt's office was ajar. Zoey slowed down when she heard a woman's voice.

"...I don't consider causing someone's death a harmless act of teenage rebellion, do you, Pastor Wilde?"

Dead silence had followed the question.

No, no, no.

The air emptied out of Zoey's lungs, making it difficult to take a breath.

She should have told Matt when she had the opportunity, but when he'd asked her to direct the cantata, she assumed it meant that he knew about her past. And he wanted her to be involved anyway.

She should have known better.

Matt's response, when it came, had been too low for her to hear.

But it didn't matter. The last thing the woman said was still ringing in Zoey's ears.

You might have a lot of empty spaces in the pews on Easter morning.

She'd been afraid that working with Matt would somehow stain his reputation in the community.

Zoey took a stumbling step backward as the door opened. The woman marched off in the opposite direction without noticing her. Matt had stepped into the hallway a second later. And almost as if he sensed her presence, he turned in her direction.

The expression on Matt's face forced Zoey back another step.

Anger. Disappointment. Disbelief.

Emotions Zoey was all too familiar with, but, somehow, seeing them on Matt's face made it more difficult to bear.

She spun around, but Matt caught up to her before she could take another step.

"Come with me."

Zoey didn't resist as his hand closed gently around her arm and he tugged her the rest of the way down the hall into the sanctuary.

Matt released her and without the bracing warmth of his touch, Zoey's knees almost gave way. She latched onto the decorative wooden rail at the altar.

Matt pushed his hands into the pockets of his jeans.

"I'm sorry, Zoey."

So was she. For a few days, Zoey had enjoyed seeing the choir and teenagers work together. Laugh together. Encourage one another.

"How could...I'm..." Matt fumbled for the right word. *"Furious."* He looked surprised when he said it, as if it wasn't an emotion he was familiar with.

Zoey didn't reply, knowing he had a right to be.

"I hate it when people spread gossip." Matt's hands clenched at his sides.

His anger wasn't directed at her?

For a second, Zoey's soul savored the sweetness of that. But she knew she owed him the truth. He had asked her to direct the cantata without understanding the possible consequences it could have.

For a moment, Zoey wanted to wrap her arms around him, press her face against the solid warmth of his broad chest and not let go.

"It's not gossip." She took another step away from him instead. "Everything that Gina Galway said... it's all true."

Chapter Nineteen

Matt's breath stuck in his throat.

"I thought you knew." The resignation in Zoey's eyes reminded him of someone facing a judge. Waiting for sentencing.

"From the things you and Liz said, I gathered that you'd lived with them for a few years but I didn't know why…" Matt paused, hoping she would trust him.

"My parents left me with my grandparents when I was sixteen. I was going through a rebellious streak and they didn't know how to handle it." Zoey looked away. "Dad was asked to lead a team of missionaries to Africa and I think he accepted because he needed a fresh start. But they didn't take me with them. It was supposed to be short term, but they were asked to stay on for another six months. And then another."

Zoey wrapped her arms around her middle, as if to hold the pain inside. "By that time, I was starting my senior year of high school. Mom and Dad claimed they didn't want to uproot me again and take me away from all the friends I'd made."

The bitter edge told Matt there hadn't been many.

"You lived with Liz and Jonathan for two years?"

"It probably seemed like a hundred to them." Zoey's smile didn't reach her eyes. "But they were amazing. I didn't appreciate how difficult it must have been to take me in. They were retired. I turned their peaceful life upside down."

"They loved you."

"Yes, but Gina was right—I didn't deserve it. I broke the rules. Got into trouble. Did everything I could think of…"

"To get your parents' attention," Matt finished.

Something flickered in Zoey's eyes. Surprise? "I didn't realize that at the time. As it got closer to graduation, I started to make up all these scenarios in my head. Mom and Dad would be so proud of me when I received my diploma. As a graduation gift, they would surprise me with a plane ticket to go back to Africa with them."

Matt guessed what was coming next, and his hands curled into fists.

"Two days before the ceremony, Dad called and said there was a glitch in their travel plans and they couldn't make it back." Zoey's voice dropped to a whisper. "I didn't…handle it well."

"I'm not sure many eighteen-year-olds would have."

"I went to a party that night. Tyler, a guy I'd had a crush on for months, was there. He was a star athlete—everyone loved him. We left together and Tyler drank too much." Zoey swallowed hard. "We ran off the road and hit a tree. I was wearing my seatbelt. Tyler wasn't. People blamed me. They didn't think it was fair that I had a few broken ribs and Tyler... died."

Matt felt sick. "You were driving?"

"No."

"Then how was the accident your fault?" he asked quietly.

Zoey twisted her fingers together. "I tried to take the keys away from Tyler but he was angry with me and wouldn't let me drive. I should have insisted. Or walked home. Something."

"Tyler was drinking and got behind the wheel of a car. You could have *both* been killed." The thought of Zoey's life cut short at the age of eighteen made Matt's stomach pitch.

"Tyler had this squeaky-clean reputation. I didn't. People assumed that I provided the beer."

People assumed.

"But you didn't." It wasn't a question.

A heartbeat of silence. "No."

"Did you explain that?"

"No one would have believed me," Zoey said with heart-wrenching honesty. "Tyler was an only child. If his parents knew that he was the one who had gotten the alcohol and that he..."

The rest of the sentence broke off.

"That he what?"

Zoey sidestepped the question. "When I got out of the hospital, I packed up my suitcase and left."

Matt sent up a silent prayer for wisdom. The haunted look in Zoey's eyes told him that there was more to the story. Things she had never shared because she didn't think anyone would believe her…and she hadn't wanted to damage Tyler Curtis's memory.

Matt reached out to take her hand, but Zoey pulled away.

"I thought for sure that you knew…that someone would have told you. Otherwise I never would have agreed to direct the cantata."

Matt's lips flattened. Several people had tried, but he'd shut down the conversation right away. The only reason Gina Galway had managed to be the one to enlighten him was because she had taken him by surprise. "I don't encourage gossip. And Liz was thrilled when you moved in with her. To me, that's what counted."

"I'll talk to Diana Riggs tomorrow about taking over for me."

"You're stepping down?"

"The only reason I agreed to take over for Gran was because I thought you knew…about me."

"I do know about you," Matt said firmly. "I know that you've already put in hours of rehearsal and the

kids in the choir would be devastated if you quit now.
I know that God has given you an amazing gift when
it comes to music and He wants you to share it."

Zoey was shaking her head. "You heard Gina.
People aren't going to want to see me at the front of
a church, reminding them of the past."

"Before you make that decision, will you promise
to do something for me?"

Zoey eyed him warily. "What?"

"When is your next practice?"

"Tomorrow night at six."

"Okay." Matt nodded. "That's about twenty-four
hours from now. Take that time and pray about it.
Ask God what you should do."

"Matt, I have to go. I promised Haylie that I would
meet her at the Grapevine."

"Promise me."

Zoey wouldn't meet his eyes. "I'll pray about it."

The door closed behind her, and Matt leaned
against the wall.

He had no doubt that Zoey would pray about it.
But he was also afraid she had already made up her
mind.

Zoey parked in front of the Grapevine. The closed
sign was in the window, but through it, she could see
Haylie sitting in a corner booth.

At least, Zoey thought, she didn't have to explain
the reason she was crying.

Because she wasn't.

The tears had crystallized inside of her before they had a chance to escape.

Gina Galway's tirade had not only reminded her what she'd done and that she didn't belong in Mirror Lake, it had also reminded Zoey who she could never belong *to*.

Matt.

While Zoey had been falling in love with him, she had somehow forgotten that someone with a past like hers could never have a future with a man like him. In a small town like Mirror Lake, it would always get in the way...

"Zoey!" Haylie stood up and waved as Zoey walked in, as if she might not spot her in the empty cafe.

"Hi, Haylie." Zoey forced a smile. She could fall apart later, in the privacy of her bedroom. Right now, Haylie was the one who mattered. "Is everything all right?"

"Everything is great." Haylie's eyes were red-rimmed but shining.

Zoey slid into the booth opposite her. "Should I take you back to your house so we can talk? I think the cafe is going to close pretty soon."

"No, it's not!" Kate sailed through the double doors that separated the dining area from the kitchen and deposited a chocolate cake in the center of the table. "I'm staying open late tonight because a celebration is in order."

"What are we celebrating?" Zoey asked.

Haylie's expression turned shy. "I thought about what you said...and I wanted to tell you that I believe it...for *me*."

Now the tears began to fall. "That is a reason to celebrate."

The next day, Matt stopped over at Liz's after work and found her in the kitchen, pouring two cups of coffee.

Relief shot through him.

That meant Zoey was here.

Earlier that morning, Matt had received a call from Angela Cornell, inviting him over for a few hours. Derek had been released from the hospital the day before, so Matt had spent the majority of the afternoon sitting on a threadbare sofa, playing video games with Derek.

He'd stopped by the church after that, hoping to catch Zoey before she left. Practice was in full swing, but there was no sign of Zoey. All Delia had been able to tell was that Zoey had called and asked her to take over.

"Here you go." Liz handed him one of the cups.

Matt stared down at the steaming liquid. The coffee was for him? "Where—"

"She's gone, Matthew," Liz said softly.

"Where is she?" He was almost afraid to ask. "I really need to talk to her."

Liz drew him over to the table. "Her boss called this afternoon. Zoey's understudy had a family emergency, so he asked if she could perform tonight."

"So she left? Just like that?" Matt couldn't believe it.

"She didn't have a choice," Liz said gently. "She has a job. Responsibilities."

But not a home, which Matt suspected was what Zoey longed for the most.

"But…" He plowed a hand through his hair, wondering how much he should tell her. "I didn't get a chance to talk to her about last night."

Liz's lips compressed. "Gina Galway."

"She told you?"

"Zoey was…quite upset when she came in last night."

Matt didn't have to close his eyes to see the stricken look on Zoey's face after she'd overheard their conversation. "Zoey thought I already knew the details of what happened."

"Maybe I should have told you." Liz sighed. "But I wanted you to form your own opinion of Zoey, based on who she is now, not on her past."

"Zoey is amazing," Matt said instantly. "She's smart. Compassionate. Funny. Creative."

Liz smiled now. "You *do* know her."

"I know she doesn't deserve condemnation from people like Gina Galway. The accident wasn't even her fault." Matt pushed to his feet, unable to sit still any longer.

"People were quick to believe the worst of her," Liz admitted. "Zoey was a handful when she came to live with us, but she was never malicious or cruel. Tyler's parents blamed Zoey for being a bad influence on their son, but I always thought there was more to the story. Something she wouldn't tell me or her grandpa."

Matt thought so, too.

He had lain awake for hours during the night, trying to piece together the details. Not only from the things Zoey had told him, but also from the ones she hadn't.

According to Zoey, everyone loved Tyler Curtis.

He had probably been a lot like Matt at that age. Loving the attention. Taking what he thought he deserved…and not caring if he hurt someone in the process as long as it made him feel good.

Matt guessed that Tyler had supplied the beer for a private party with Zoey and then became upset when she didn't live up to *her* reputation.

She blamed herself for not doing more to stop him from driving, and she didn't want to stain his memory by telling people the truth. That Tyler had been drunk, angry with her and driving too fast when he lost control of his vehicle.

"What I don't understand," Matt said tightly, "is why she separated herself from her parents and from you and Jonathan after it happened? She cut herself off from the people who loved her because of something that wasn't even her fault. It doesn't make sense."

"She felt as if she let everyone down." Liz's shoulders drooped. "I love my son and daughter-in-law dearly, but they were hard on Zoey when she was growing up. It was Paul's first church and he was so careful to do everything right. He wanted to be the perfect pastor. The perfect husband. The perfect father.

"Zoey told me one Christmas that she felt like she lived under a microscope. I wish I would have taken her more seriously." Liz's eyes darkened with regret. "I should have talked to Paul about how difficult it was for her."

Each word landed like a blow.

Matt finally understood the reason why Zoey seemed to shy away from him. Not because she didn't feel the attraction between them, but because she *did*. She was protecting herself. A man like him, involved in full-time ministry, would be the last person Zoey would want to be with.

It was an obstacle that Matt hadn't seen. Until now.

"Paul and Sara were very strict with her," Liz continued. "I think they were so afraid she would rebel, they wouldn't allow her the simple freedoms that other girls her age enjoyed."

"So she rebelled." Matt knew that it happened. "And they sent her to Mirror Lake."

"It was only supposed to be for six months."

"Then why didn't they take Zoey with them?" Matt

wanted to hear Liz's perspective on the situation, to see if it meshed with what Zoey felt.

"They honestly believed they were doing the right thing by leaving her in the States. Paul and Sara would have had to leave her in a mission school for half the time." The memories drove Liz to her feet, and she walked over to the coffee pot to refill Matt's cup.

"But they aren't the only ones to blame. Jonathan and I agreed that Zoey would be better off with us, too. She loved coming to visit us for a week in the summer and…" Liz hesitated. "I hoped that Zoey would feel a…a burden lifted. She could be herself here. But it didn't work out that way. Zoey felt abandoned.

"In the spring before she graduated, I began to see some positive changes in her. Paul and Sara planned to come back for the commencement ceremony and Zoey had received a music scholarship for a college in the southern part of the state. She was devastated when her parents called and told us there was a glitch in their travel plans and they weren't going to be able to make it back. The accident happened that night. Tyler's car hit a tree near the lake. He died at the scene and Zoey…"

"She was injured?" Matt's gut twisted at the thought of Zoey in pain.

"She spent a few days in the hospital with a mild concussion and some other injuries. When the doctor signed her release papers, she came back here, packed up her things and left." Liz's eyes clouded with the memory. "We got a letter from her a few weeks later. She said it would be best if she severed all contact." Liz's voice broke. "But she meant it would be best for us, not for her."

Matt listened with a growing sense of dread as Liz's words began to sink in.

He remembered the veiled warning Gina Galway had made right before she'd left.

Zoey would have heard it, too.

"Gina hinted that the turnout might not be as good this year if Zoey was the director."

"She might be right," Liz said evenly. "There are always people who don't believe that God has the power to change peoples' lives. Zoey needs to understand that for every person like Gina Galway and Rose Williams, there are people who understand the meaning of grace."

Matt knew that Zoey did.

He remembered her compassionate response to Haylie. She hadn't judged her. She hadn't pointed a finger at her—she'd pointed to God.

If he was half as brave as she was, he wouldn't have shied away from talking to Rob because it stirred up his own past. A past he wasn't proud of. A past he had never shared with anyone because, like Zoey's father, he had wanted peoples' respect.

"Well, I don't care how many people come to the cantata. I care about Zoey." Who was he kidding? It didn't begin to describe the depths of his feelings. He *loved* her. "And when she comes back, I'm going to tell her that."

Something in Liz's expression tipped him off. The truth slammed into him.

"You don't think she's going to come back," he said flatly.

"I hope she does."

Matt couldn't find much comfort in that. "But the cantata...she's put so much time and energy into it. She can't just walk away from that."

She can't walk away from me.

"She might." Liz's eyes misted over. "If she thinks that coming back here will hurt you."

Chapter Twenty

"I had a hunch you'd be hiding in here."

"I'm not hiding, Mel. I'm getting ready for the performance." To prove it to her friend, Zoey bent down to lace up the pink high-top tennis shoes she wore in the opening scene.

"It's more than an hour to curtain time." Melissa collapsed in one of the tulip-shaped beanbag chairs and tugged the ruffles on her red taffeta skirt over her knees.

Zoey froze as her cell phone suddenly came to life, belting out the opening line of one of her favorite songs.

"Your phone is ringing," Melissa said helpfully.

"I know." It was the third time Zoey had heard it ring in the past hour. And she'd ignored it every time.

Melissa scooped it up and squinted at the tiny screen. "Matthew Wilde."

Zoey's heart flipped over at the sound of his name.

If she actually heard his voice, she would probably go into cardiac arrest.

"I know."

"Why don't you want to talk to him?"

"I have to finish getting ready," Zoey reminded her.

Melissa pulled a silver feather duster out of the pocket of her satin tunic and pointed it in her direction. "Don't make me use this."

"You take your role as my fairy godmother way too seriously."

"I'm supposed to get into character." Melissa grinned. "So who is this Matthew Wilde? And why won't you talk to him? You haven't said much since you got into town yesterday."

"I haven't had a lot of time," Zoey pointed out. "I walked in two hours before curtain."

Scott had practically begged her to come back and take her rightful place as Ella for the evening performance. Tina, Zoey's understudy, had been called home for a family emergency.

After the curtain call, Scott had pulled her aside. Tina left a message on his machine, requesting another day off. Which meant Zoey would have to stay in the Dells and postpone her trip back to Mirror Lake another day.

Matt had encouraged her to pray about directing the cantata and Zoey wondered if the delay wasn't her answer. Now she would have a little more time to decide if she would go back at all.

Gran's last appointment with Dr. Parish had gone well. So well, in fact, that he'd lifted all his prior restrictions and told Liz she could go back to her usual routine. Everyone involved in the cantata knew their parts, and Delia was more than capable of making sure it went smoothly on Easter morning.

The best thing to do, Zoey reasoned, was to step back and be content that she'd done everything she needed to do.

Melissa leaned forward and waved the feather duster under her nose. "Earth to Zoey."

Zoey's sigh released a puff of glitter into the air. "He's the pastor of my grandmother's church, nosy."

Melissa's kohl-rimmed eyes widened. "And you aren't answering the phone? What if something is wrong…why are you blushing?"

"I'm *not* blushing. I'm probably allergic to glitter."

"Uh huh." Melissa sounded skeptical. "So, your grandma's pastor—Matthew Wilde—is calling, but you aren't answering it even though there could be an emergency—"

"There's no emergency," Zoey ground out.

"So what does he want?"

Zoey wished she knew.

"I guess he wants to…talk to me."

Melissa tapped the feather duster against her knee and released another cloud of glitter into the air. She frowned."I know you weren't looking forward to going back to Mirror Lake because of everything that happened. Has he been giving you a hard time?"

"Mel, Matt is…he's been great, okay?"

More than great.

She'd told him everything and it hadn't seemed to make a difference. The censure she'd once been so afraid of seeing in his eyes had never appeared. Just the opposite. He'd looked as if he'd wanted to take her into his arms…

"You're blushing again."

"I am not." A glance in the mirror above the dressing table told Zoey that yes, she was.

Melissa's mouth fell open. "I don't believe this. You like this guy. Admit it."

Zoey crossed her arms. "Are we in sixth grade?"

"Is he young? Good looking?"

"What does that have to do with anything?"

The feather duster slashed an arch through the air like a sword. "Just answer the question."

"Which one?"

"Zoey—"

"Fine. Yes and yes. But it's not what you're thinking," Zoey added quickly. "Matt wants me to come back and direct the Easter cantata, that's all." She rose to her feet but there was no room to pace in the cramped dressing area.

"Direct the…" Melissa's voice trailed off. "You have been keeping secrets."

You have no idea, Zoey tamped down a sigh.

"Sit down. You're making me dizzy," her friend

commanded. When Zoey complied, she leaned forward. "Now tell Melissa everything."

So Zoey did. She told her about meeting Matthew on the road the day she'd arrived. Her emotional reunion with Gran. The knitting club. The way Matt had willingly given up George. The youth group. Finding Gran on the floor. Matt volunteering her to take Gran's place for the Easter cantata. Her conversation with Haylie.

When Zoey got to the part about overhearing Gina Galway's confrontation with Matt, Melissa looked troubled.

"You aren't the same person you were then."

"To people like Gina Galway I am."

"You need to read Psalm 40 again." Melissa got up and retrieved the extra Bible she knew Zoey kept on a shelf in the dressing room.

"Now?"

"Humor me."

"Is there going to be a quiz afterward?" Zoey muttered.

Melissa didn't crack a smile. "Maybe."

Zoey thumbed through the pages until she found the psalm that she and Melissa had studied together six months ago. The same one that Matt had chosen as a sermon topic.

Was God trying to tell her something?

"I waited patiently for the Lord. He turned to me and heard my cry. He lifted me out of the slimy pit, out of the mud and the mire, he set my feet on a rock and gave me a firm place to stand…" The letters blurred and Zoey stopped reading.

"Keep going," Melissa prompted.

"He put a new song in my mouth, a hymn of praise to our God. Many will see and fear and put their trust in the Lord."

"It says that people will trust in God when they see a changed life. A new song. But no one is going to hear it unless you sing it," Melissa said. "You left Mirror Lake when you were eighteen because you thought it was the right thing to do, Zoey. Don't you think that maybe the right thing to do this time is *stay?*"

A tap on the door prevented Zoey from having to respond.

"You don't want to keep Brit waiting, ladies," a voice on the other side called out cheerfully. "Time to put your faces on."

"Thanks, Mike." Zoey closed the Bible and put it back on the shelf. "Tell her we'll be right there."

The phone rang again as they walked to the door. Zoey and Melissa both turned to stare at it but this time neither of them picked it up.

"Zoey girl…"

"I can't go back." Until Zoey said the words, she hadn't realized there really wasn't anything more to think about.

Not only did the people in Matt's congregation love him, but he was also a respected member of the community. She couldn't risk hurting his reputation.

There would always be people like Gina Galway. There were those who had criticized her parents, held them responsible for the mistakes Zoey had made. She couldn't do that to Matt.

"Because of one woman who is holding a grudge." Melissa glowered at her.

Zoey thought about Rose Williams and some of the others in Matt's congregation whose stony expressions told her that they hadn't forgotten. "I doubt it's only one."

"There are always going to be people who look at the speck in someone's eye and ignore the log in their own, as Jesus said," Melissa said. "It sounds to me like Zoey Decker has touched a lot of people in Mirror Lake. Her grandmother. Haylie Owens. Delia Peake…"

Zoey laughed. "I wouldn't go that far."

"And don't forget Matt," Melissa added.

It would be impossible to forget Matt.

Zoey had done everything in her power to prevent it, but in the past few weeks, everything about him had become imprinted on her heart.

She was falling in love with Matt. The last thing Zoey wanted to do was hurt him.

"Matt?" Kate knocked on the door of his office. "Do you have a second?"

"Sure."

"Follow me."

Matt scraped up a smile and trailed after Kate, down the hall to the youth room.

Zoey still hadn't returned. According to Liz, she had called that morning and explained that her boss had asked her to stay an extra day.

Matt wasn't sure what to do. Zoey wouldn't return his phone calls. It looked as if Liz was right. The emergency at work had provided the perfect opportunity to step back from the cantata. And, if Liz's theory was on target, from him. Zoey didn't plan on coming back to Mirror Lake.

Kate linked her arm through his. "This will only take a few minutes."

"What's going on?"

"An ambush." Kate grinned. "But don't worry. It's friendly-fire."

"Friendly…" Matt's voice was drowned out by a piercing whistle. A dozen teenagers snapped to attention.

"Told you." Kate stepped back as they surrounded him.

Matt's gaze swept over the group. "Why aren't you in school?"

"Spring break," Tim Davis said.

Now Matt understood. Kate must have planned a get-together at the church. He had been drafted to round out a team for game time in the past. Matt wasn't exactly in the mood to play, but then again, it might take his mind off Zoey. "Scavenger hunt? Capture the Flag?"

"Better." Morgan stepped forward and held out a slim white envelope. "We have something for you."

Matt eyed it warily. "My birthday isn't until October."

"Just open it!" one of the girls sang out. There was a chorus of agreement and everyone pressed closer as Matt pulled out a colorful strip of paper.

"A ticket?"

"To a play," Zach Davis said.

Matt tried to muster some enthusiasm. Plays reminded him of Zoey.

Who was he kidding?

Everything reminded him of Zoey.

"Thanks." Matt saw the expectant looks on their faces and sensed they were waiting for something. "Um…what play?"

"It's called *'Once Upon a Castle,'*" Morgan said, a smug look on her face.

Once Upon a Castle.

"But that's…"

"Zoey's play," Rob finished. He didn't look the least bit guilty over his involvement in the scheme.

Matt frowned. "Why would you get me a ticket to see Zoey's play?"

"At practice last night, Delia said that Zoey might not come back." Morgan parked her hands on her hips.

"She can't miss the cantata." Haylie Owens stepped forward, shy but determined. "We *need* her. And we think you should go get her."

A murmur of agreement followed the statement.

Matt needed Zoey, too. And he'd been praying for an opportunity to tell her.

He looked down at the ticket.

You always do the unexpected, don't You, Lord?

"When is it?"

Kate glanced at her watch. "In five hours."

"It's tonight?" Matt's eyebrows shot up.

"It has to be," Tim Davis pointed out.

Matt knew the boy was right. They were running out of time. The cantata was Sunday, Easter morning. God, with a little help from the Church of the Pines youth group, had given him a small—a very small—window of opportunity to convince Zoey to come back.

Who was he to question it?

"If you leave in the next half hour, you'll make it there with fifteen minutes to spare." Kate saw his dazed expression and shrugged. "I printed out the directions."

Matt released a slow smile. "I think I can manage that."

Zach and Tim's hands connected in a high five. "Yes!"

After the play, Matt would invite Zoey out for a cup of coffee. Find a quiet, private corner in a restaurant...

"Um, Pastor Matt?"

Matt's eyes narrowed when he saw a guilty look chase across Morgan's face. "What is it?"

"The ticket we bought for you…it's kind of a special one."

"A special one," Matt repeated. He glanced at the slip of paper and noticed a little gold emblem stamped in the corner. "What does the crown mean? I get a table in the front?"

"Kind of," Rob muttered.

Tim sank an elbow into his friend's ribs.

"Ten minutes and counting." Kate pointed at the door and set the collection of metal bracelets on her wrist into motion.

Matt's gaze swept over the teenagers and his throat felt tight.

"Thanks, guys."

"Break a leg, Pastor Matt!" Zach shouted.

Everyone laughed. "Yeah, break a leg, Pastor."

"What does that mean?" he muttered to Kate.

Kate's green eyes danced with laughter. "It means they expect to see Zoey tomorrow."

Zoey and tomorrow.

Matt decided that he liked the sound of those two words together.

Chapter Twenty-One

"Hold still, Zoey, or I'm going to tie you to this chair."

Brit, the makeup girl, attacked Zoey's cheeks with a sable brush almost the size of Melissa's feather duster. "Why so jittery? I heard that last night's performance went great."

Zoey closed her eyes as a cloud of beige face powder mushroomed into the air around them.

She wished she could shrug off her restlessness as stage fright. But Zoey knew that if she followed it to its source, she would find her feelings for Matt at the center.

Melissa breezed in. "My turn."

"What do you think, Mel?" Brit eyed Zoey the way an artist would a painting that hadn't turned out quite right. "I covered up the dark circles but I can't seem to do anything about the lovesick, puppy dog look in her eyes."

Zoey groaned. "Melissa."

"I didn't say a word."

"Process of elimination," Brit said. "If stage fright or a double shot of espresso didn't put that look in your eyes, it has to be love."

"Very funny." Zoey slid off the chair and stripped off the towel that had been protecting her costume. She wore the same pair of faded blue jeans and tennis shoes she had been wearing the first time she'd met Matt.

"You're thinking about him again."

With a start, Zoey realized that Brit had left. Melissa stood near the door, arms folded over her chest.

"No." It wasn't a lie. Because the truth was, Zoey hadn't *stopped* thinking about Matt.

There was a tap on the door. "Ready, Zoey?"

"Lead the way, Mike."

Melissa reeled her in for a quick hug as she walked by. "Smile." Her eyes matched the sequins in her dress for sparkle. "You're about to meet your prince, remember?"

A smile tugged at Zoey's lips. The last performance, her "prince" had been seventy-five years old and while they'd waltzed together, he'd whispered in Zoey's ear that he was considered quite a catch in the senior apartment complex where he lived.

Because the play encouraged audience participation, ushers stood on either side of the stage with "cues" written on large pieces of tag board. Most parts were cast as people took their seats, but the important roles—Zoey's "stepmother," her two stepsisters and the prince—were often purchased in advance by people who wanted a friend or family member featured in a more prominent role.

Those characters were given a simple, one-page script attached to a clipboard. Part of Zoey's job—and that of the cue card holders—was to generate laughter and make sure the characters said their lines at the right time. Fortunately, those two things usually went hand in hand.

Zoey took her place behind the heavy velvet curtain as the lights in the theatre dimmed. The hum of conversation and the clink of dishes subsided. The orchestra launched into "Until I Met You."

It was the song Zoey had been practicing the day Gina Galway had shown up.

The day she'd realized that she was in love with Matt.

The usher chuckled when Matt showed him his ticket.

"Brit!" He waved to someone lurking in the shadows. "Here's your guy."

Before Matt could blink, a young woman appeared and whisked him behind the stage area down a narrow, dimly lit corridor, walking faster in stilettos than Matt could in his favorite pair of Nikes.

"Where are we going?" Matt looked around, hoping to get a glimpse of Zoey.

"Costume," the mysterious woman named Brit said as she ushered him into a small room.

"Costume?"

"You're Elliot Charming. Aka the prince."

"I don't think so." Matt laughed.

Brit didn't.

She pulled a black tuxedo jacket off a portable rack in the corner of the dressing room and held it up, silently measuring it against the width of Matt's shoulders. "Gold crown in the corner of your ticket?"

"Yes."

"The ticket is kind of a special one," he remembered Morgan saying.

Matt winced.

Thanks, guys.

"Then you're it. *Him.*" Brit sounded way too cheerful as she pushed him down into a chair and turned to a tray of instruments that looked more intimidating than the ones Matt had seen in the dentist office.

In less than sixty seconds, he was back on his feet. And afraid to look at his reflection in the mirror.

"Listen—" Matt knew he sounded a little desperate. He'd been hoping to alert Zoey to his presence before the performance started, but a fender bender involving two minivans at an intersection had eaten up eleven minutes of the extra fifteen Kate had promised him. "I need to talk to Zoey Decker."

Brit snapped her gum and held out the tux. "Put this on."

"My name is Matt Wilde." He wrangled one arm into the sleeve. "Can you at least tell her that I'm here?"

Brit adjusted the silk handkerchief in Matt's pocket and gave him a gentle shove. "Honey, walk straight through that curtain and you can tell her yourself."

There was no time to escape. A stagehand spotted Matt and waved him over.

"Here's the prince." The guy pressed a clipboard into his hands. "Don't look so nervous. This is going to be easy. Walk across the stage toward the dark-haired girl—she's your Cinderella, by the way—and read the first line of the script. We'll take care of the rest."

The words on the paper began to dance.

"Three, two…you're on, Mr. Charming."

Somehow, Matt got his legs to work.

Light applause and a few whistles drowned out the song she was singing as Matt stepped onto the stage.

According to the script, Zoey was supposed to tip over the bucket. That was Matt's cue to say his line.

Matt looked down at the clipboard again.

PRINCE CHARMING: CAN I HELP YOU?

He should be able to handle that. He hoped. The closer he got to Zoey, the more uncertain he became.

Until this moment, Matt hadn't realized that everything about Zoey had become imprinted on his heart. The cherry-cola curls that framed her delicate face. The sweep of dark lashes. The curve of her jaw…

Metallic-blue confetti from the overturned bucket

next to Zoey fluttered toward his boots. His hiking boots. He was wearing a formal tux and *hiking boots.*

If it didn't involve breaking one of the ten commandments, Matt could have cheerfully killed Kate Nichols, along with the rest of the well-meaning kids in the youth group.

He cleared his throat. "Can I help you?"

Zoey looked up and the smile died on her face.

According to the script, she was supposed to say 'No, thank you."

But she didn't say anything.

Not a single word. She just stared up at him in disbelief.

"No, thank you." Matt mouthed her line.

Zoey blinked. "What are you doing here?"

Out of the corner of his eye, Matt saw the guy holding the cue card shake his head.

This wasn't good. He was supposed to be talking to Zoey over a cup of coffee in a quiet restaurant… *not* ruining her performance.

"NO, THANK YOU," a stagehand whispered loudly.

Zoey rose to her feet. "No, thank you," she repeated with a wide smile.

Relief poured through Matt. Until he glanced down and noticed the word SMILE in the script.

Then he saw the next line.

EXIT PRINCE.

Matt decided it would probably be a good idea.

* * *

Zoey wasn't quite sure how, but she managed to make it through the performance.

Matt, who had looked as if he'd been struck dumb by the spotlight, discovered his inner fairy tale prince halfway through Act One. By the time Ella Cinders and Elliot Charming met again at the dance studio, Matt had the entire audience laughing uproariously every time he twitched an eyebrow or pretended to sneeze whenever Melissa pointed the feather duster at him.

The fact that he looked spectacular in a tux didn't hurt, either.

In the final scene, Zoey came out wearing her ball gown. It was her favorite costume, a cloud of white satin, seed pearls and miles of delicate lace. The toes of her pink high tops peeked out beneath the hem.

When Matt's eyes met hers, Zoey forgot her next line again. Their eyes met as he took her hand. But instead of going down on one knee and professing his undying love for her the way the prince was supposed to do, Matt drew her gently into his arms.

His hand traced the curve of Zoey's jaw. She would have looked away but Matt's fingers curved under her chin and he lifted her face. In the warm depths of his hazel eyes, Zoey saw her reflection. And something else, too. Something unexpected that weakened her knees.

Something that looked like…a promise.

Before Zoey had time to think—to tell herself that

she was imagining things—Matt lowered his head and his lips touched hers in a tender, almost reverent kiss.

Zoey's heart almost stopped beating.

"That's not in the script," she heard one of the extras muttered.

Zoey felt Matt smile.

And then he kissed her again.

Applause erupted from the audience, who obviously thought the show was over.

The stagehand standing in the wings tossed the cue cards into the air and walked away.

Matt's breath stirred the curls near Zoey's ear.

"If we leave right after the performance, we'll be back in Mirror Lake by midnight."

Zoey had a long car ride to think about that kiss.

As she followed Matt's truck back to Mirror Lake, she felt a little like Ella Cinders, who had found love when she least expected it. With the kind of man she'd only dreamed of.

Except in Zoey's dream, the man she'd dreamed of hadn't been a pastor.

She still wasn't sure she was doing the right thing. She and Matt hadn't had a lot of time to talk after the performance, but he had explained that the youth group had bought the ticket for tonight's performance.

"You've worked so hard to put this together. The

kids want you to be there," Matt had said. "And so do I."

How could she say no?

As Zoey passed the Mirror Lake city limits sign, it seemed like months, rather than weeks, had passed since she'd first laid eyes on that sign and pulled over to the side of the road. And met Matt.

Everything had changed except the panic that pressed down on her, making it difficult to breathe.

You're going to have to help me, Lord.

As Zoey followed Matt through town, his truck slowed down to make a right turn onto Carriage Street.

At the end of the block, lights blazed from the windows in Gran's house and Zoey saw an unfamiliar vehicle parked in the driveway. It was just after midnight and Liz never stayed up past the ten o'clock news.

Zoey wrenched the Jeep into park and opened the door. Matt was at her side the moment her feet hit the ground.

"I'm sure everything is fine or someone would have called," he said reassuringly.

"If Gran *let* them call," Zoey pointed out, remembering that Liz didn't like to be, in her words, "a bother."

"Gran?" Zoey felt Matt take her hand as she dashed inside.

"We're in the parlor, sweetheart." Liz's lilting response made it a little easy to breathe.

"Who's in the parlor with her?" she whispered.

"I have no idea," Matt whispered back. "I didn't recognize the car."

Zoey sidestepped George as she entered the room and almost lost her balance. Matt reached out to steady her.

"Hello, Zoey."

Zoey's knees turned to liquid and she must have swayed because Matt's grip on her hand tightened.

The man and woman who'd been sitting next to Gran on the sofa rose slowly to their feet.

"They just arrived an hour ago," Liz said, her brown eyes beseeching as they met Zoey's.

"We wanted to surprise you." The woman took a hesitant step forward and then stopped, her eyes uncertain as they met Zoey's.

"Paul and Sara, this is the pastor of my church." Liz stood up, too. "Matthew, I'd like you to meet my son and his wife."

Matt looked down at her, a question in his eyes.

Zoey nodded stiffly and tried to work up a smile. "My parents."

Chapter Twenty-Two

Zoey skipped breakfast the next morning and slipped out of the house while everyone was still asleep. When she walked into the sanctuary, she found a whirlwind of activity instead of a quiet place to contemplate everything that had happened over the past twenty-four hours—and to recover from the shock of seeing her parents again.

If it hadn't been for the warmth of Matt's hand, infusing her with strength, she would never have made it through the awkward silence that fell after the introductions.

Gran had come to the rescue, reminding everyone that it was late and how a good night's sleep made a difference.

Zoey wasn't sure what *kind* of difference her grandmother meant, but she took advantage of the suggestion. With a mumbled "goodnight," she'd fled.

Matt must have sensed how close she was to falling apart because he didn't try to stop her.

For the next hour, Zoey lay awake in bed, listening to the soft murmur of voices in the guest room next to hers. Her parents' voices.

Zoey could only imagine why they were there. Were they worried about Liz? Had they found out that Zoey was staying there and decided to fly back from Africa to check on things?

That seemed to be the more likely reason for the surprise visit.

"Zoey!" Someone spotted her and all activity ceased.

For the next half hour, Zoey was mobbed. She admired the set. Listened to the opening notes of Trudy Kimball's flute solo and wrote down the ingredients of a sore throat remedy for Morgan, who had strained her vocal cords while practicing at home the day before.

Haylie pulled Zoey aside when the others returned to their tasks.

"How are you doing?" Zoey asked, even though the girl's bright expression provided a clue.

"Good." Haylie grinned. "Now. We were all a little worried when we heard you had to leave."

Zoey noticed Rob watching them. Haylie followed the direction of her gaze and turned pink. "We had a long talk." Her voice dropped. "I told Rob what you said about not being able to change the past, but we both want our relationship to be…different. And you know what? Pastor Matt said the same thing you did. That God will help us."

Haylie sounded a little amazed by that. To be honest, Zoey was often a little amazed by it, too.

Something else the girl said suddenly registered.

"Pastor Matt talked to Rob?"

"Uh-huh. He didn't tell me everything they said because it's *guy stuff.*" Haylie shook her head. "But whatever it was, Rob said that he wants to trust God with his future. And he doesn't want to do anything to mess up His plans for me either."

"Wow." Zoey couldn't think of anything else to say.

"That's what I thought." Haylie smiled. "They are going to meet for Bible study once a week. I was wondering if you and I…if you'd do that with me."

Zoey sat down on the piano bench. How could she commit to meeting with the girl on a regular basis when she planned to leave Mirror Lake in a few days?

"We'll talk later." For now, it was the only promise she could make.

"Okay." Haylie skipped toward Morgan. The two girls began to set up music stands together and it became obvious there was a friendship in the making.

Thank You, God.

Kate pressed a cup of coffee into her hand. "You look like you could use this."

"Thanks."

"For the coffee or for sending Matt to get you?" Kate's shamrock eyes sparkled.

Until now, Zoey had had no idea that Kate master-minded the scheme. It shredded her theory that Matt and the cafe owner were interested in each other.

But then again, so had Matt's kiss…

If Melissa were there, she would accuse Zoey of blushing again.

Kate cleared her throat and Zoey realized she was waiting for an answer.

"Right now, for the coffee," she said. "I'll let you know about the other one after the cantata tomorrow."

"It's going to be great."

Zoey wished she could be sure. It suddenly occurred to her that she'd been concerned about how many people might *not* attend the service instead of the two she knew who would be there.

Her parents.

She continued to pray for wisdom, but Zoey still wasn't sure what to do. Everyone assumed that her arrival meant she was still planning to direct the can-tata, but Zoey couldn't stop thinking about the terrible things Gina had said. The threats she'd made.

Was it fair to jeopardize Matt's standing in the community? To undermine the respect his congrega-tion had for him?

"Hey, you two!" Abby breezed up to them, a wicker basket tucked under her arm. "It looks beautiful in here."

Kate leaned closer and sniffed the air. "Pecan pie?"

"I used your recipe." Abby grinned. "I made two for the potluck dinner this evening."

"I haven't had time to make a thing yet," Kate confessed. "It doesn't start until six, right? That means I still have time."

"So, where is the potluck?" Zoey asked.

Kate and Abby exchanged looks.

"Uh...*here*," Kate finally said. "Because of the cantata, we don't have a sunrise breakfast like a lot of churches—we host a potluck meal the night before. It's an annual tradition."

To Zoey, it was another obstacle in her path.

"No one mentioned it." Not even Gran. But maybe like the others, her grandmother had assumed Zoey remembered the event.

"Emma and I are on the hostess committee, but we decided not to ask you to bring something because you've been busy enough with the music," Abby explained. "There is usually a good turnout from the community."

The innocent comment was another reminder that because of her, there might not be a good turnout from the community. Or from the rest of the church, for that matter.

"I'm sure you'll have a good time," Zoey murmured.

"You aren't coming?"

And risk a scene with someone like Rose Williams or one of her friends? "I don't think so."

Kate frowned as if something else had occurred to

her. "If no one mentioned the potluck, does that mean you didn't hear about the special music?"

"Special music?" Zoey echoed.

"Every year someone performs a piece from the cantata. You know, kind of a sneak peak before the service tomorrow morning."

Zoey stifled a groan. "No one mentioned that either."

"Maybe Delia is taking care of it," Kate said.

Zoey hoped so. Gran could have taken it upon herself to assign Delia or one of the other choir members to take care of that particular detail. "I'll make sure it's taken care of."

"In person, right?" Kate wasn't going to let her off the hook.

"I'm not so sure that's a good idea."

"Don't let a few people and their opinions keep you from doing what you're meant to do," Kate said softly.

Which meant she'd heard the rumors, too. Zoey shouldn't have been surprised.

"We're supposed to let our light shine, not hide it." Abby reached out and gave Zoey's hand a comforting squeeze.

Zoey knew the verse in the New Testament that her friend was referring to. But what if letting her light shine ended up casting a shadow over Matt?

Was it still the right thing to do? That's what she wasn't sure of.

"Hey, Zoey!" Zach Davis jogged up to them. "We need you."

The next hour passed quickly, and Kate decided the volunteers needed some sustenance. She took the choir members and the youth group down to the fellowship room to distribute cold drinks and snacks. Zoey stayed behind to finish the decorating.

The delicate scent of lilies hung in the air as she picked up a purple cloth to drape over the cross on the wall behind the altar.

"Let me help you." Sara Decker picked up the other end.

Zoey's father stood behind her.

Zoey swallowed the lump in her throat. Her father looked different. Streaks of silver shot through his dark hair and the African sun had turned his skin to bronze. But physical changes weren't the only ones that Zoey noticed. There was something in his eyes she didn't remember. A softness that hadn't been there before.

"We'd both like to help," Paul Decker's smooth baritone washed over her. "Your grandmother told us that you're directing the Easter cantata tomorrow."

The only thing Zoey could manage was a nod.

As if she couldn't help herself, her mother reached out and brushed a stray curl off Zoey's cheek. Zoey resisted the urge to lean into the touch.

"Gran must be so excited you're here." She strove to make her voice sound normal. "She said it's been a few years since you've been back to the States."

Her parents exchanged a glance.

When Zoey looked at her father, she was stunned to see tears in his eyes.

"That's true, honey," he said in a low voice. "But we came back to see *you*."

Zoey stared at him, speechless.

"Ten years is too long, Zoey," Sara said in a voice that shook with emotion.

"We thought we were doing the right thing by leaving you in Mirror Lake with your grandparents." Paul's eyes, the same of gray as Zoey's, took on a diamond-bright shine. "Your mother and I love you. And we hope that you can forgive us. We made a mistake."

It was the first time she had ever seen him cry.

Ten years *was* too long. And Zoey knew that she'd made a mistake, too, when she'd separated herself from the people that loved her.

"I do forgive you." Zoey took a step forward, straight into her father's arms. "But you have to forgive me, too."

Chapter Twenty-Three

❦

"I thought we saw the last of Zoey Decker, but I heard she's back. Again."

Matt paused as he heard a familiar voice rise above the pre-potluck commotion in the church kitchen.

Rose Williams.

"Someone told me that Pastor Wilde actually drove all the way to Lake Delton and *asked* her to come back."

A harrumph followed the whispered statement. "If he did, he must not know what people are saying."

Oh, Matt knew what they were saying and he didn't care. But he still wasn't sure he'd convinced Zoey of that.

Matt closed his eyes and asked God for an extra measure of patience.

Gina had accused him of being blind, but Matt remembered the simmering resentment in Rose's eyes the night he'd shown up at Liz's house to give Zoey the sermon notes. He'd asked Liz about it and discovered that Rose and Tyler Curtis's mother had been best friends. Matt understood that Rose's unresolved grief and anger needed a target but he also knew it shouldn't be Zoey.

"I heard her parents came back because they found out Zoey has been staying with Liz and they got worried about her." Another hushed voice joined the conversation.

"I would be worried, too, if I were them."

Matt's hands clenched at his sides.

"My friend, Gina, refuses to come to the service tomorrow," another woman whispered.

"I'm afraid a lot of people feel that way," Vivian Clark said. "Some of the people in my book club usually attend the Easter service, but they already said they're going to skip it this year."

"It's terrible," Rose agreed. "The way Zoey Decker just waltzes around town like she didn't do anything wrong."

Because she didn't, Matt thought. And maybe this was a good time to tell them that.

He stepped into the kitchen. "Ladies," he said evenly.

Absolute silence descended on the room.

"Pastor," one of the women finally croaked out.

Rose Williams lifted her chin. Under her defiant stare, Matt saw a woman still bound by grief. The same kind of grief that had once weighed Zoey down.

Conversation in the fellowship hall quieted and several people inched closer.

"I'm sorry you have a problem with Zoey," Matt said. "I wish you would have come and talked to me about it."

"You know I'm right about her," Rose said in a hard voice. "The accident—"

"Was just that," Matt interrupted gently. "An accident. An accident that Zoey didn't cause."

"Janet was my best friend—our boys grew up together. They were going to room together in college." Rose's voice thinned as it increased in volume. "If it wasn't for Zoey, Tyler would still be alive."

"She wasn't driving the car that night."

Rose sucked in a breath. "She provided the alcohol…"

"Zoey said that she didn't."

"And you believed her?"

"Yes," Matt said simply.

"Then why did she leave right after she got out of the hospital?" Jason, a man who worked side by side with Matt on the mentoring team, sidled up and stood next to Rose.

"Maybe she didn't think anyone would believe her side of the story," Matt said. "Or maybe she didn't want to say anything that might damage Tyler's reputation."

"*Tyler's* reputation?" Rose glared at him.

Matt hesitated, not sure how much information he should share until he had an opportunity to talk to Zoey first. He'd called Jake Sutton earlier that morning and asked him to pull up the incident report taken on the night of the accident. What he read hadn't come as a shock, but Matt knew it would to the people gathered around him.

Then he remembered the pain he'd seen in Zoey's eyes the night she'd told him about the accident. Even then, she'd tried to protect Tyler's reputation at the expense of her own. Further proof of the kind of person she was.

"Excessive speed and alcohol both contributed to the crash," Matt reminded Rose. "Zoey was in the passenger seat. She was injured, too."

"We know that," someone muttered. "She walked away with a mild concussion, a few bruises and a broken wrist."

"The concussion happened at the scene of the accident. The other injuries happened *before* the car hit the tree," Matt said softly.

"Before the accident?" Walt Jenkins' bushy eyebrows dipped together in a frown. "What do you mean?"

Matt chose his words with care. "Tyler had been drinking. He didn't appreciate Zoey cutting their… date…short that night."

Rose stared at him, wide-eyed. "That can't be… maybe Tyler had a bit of a temper when he didn't get his way, but…" She clapped a hand over her mouth when she realized what she'd been about to reveal.

Out of the corner of his eye, Matt saw several people exchange grim but knowing looks, leaving him to wonder if Tyler had been as perfect in the eyes of the town as Zoey believed.

It wasn't his intent to smear Tyler Curtis's name or shift the blame to a young man whose life had been cut short. But if there was going to finally be healing, Zoey had to stop blaming herself for something that had been out of her control. And others had to stop blaming her, too.

"She's never going to forgive me," Rose said, her eyes dark with another kind of grief. "The things I said…"

"Yes, she will," Matt said with absolute certainty.

Rose sagged against her husband. "You don't know that."

"I know Zoey."

Matt heard the stir that followed and his heart clenched. Were people still going to reject Zoey, even now that the truth had come out?

His gaze swept over the room. That's when he realized it wasn't his words that had jumpstarted another round of whispers.

It was Zoey.

Zoey's gaze collided with Matt's across the room.

Up until ten minutes ago, she hadn't even planned to attend the potluck. While her parents and Gran got ready, she'd retreated to her room.

Delia and Morgan had agreed to perform their duet for the potluck. Everything was in place for the Easter service the following morning. There was no reason for her to go…except for an overwhelming feeling that she *should*.

Zoey had quickly fixed her hair, changed into a white blouse and a lavender ballet-style skirt and caught up with her family just before her parents' rental car pulled out of the driveway.

Liz had commented on how quiet the church was as they made their way downstairs to the fellowship hall.

When Zoey heard Matt's voice, she thought they had somehow misjudged the time and he'd already started the message.

Then she realized that he was talking to Rose Williams. About her.

Zoey's knees suddenly felt as if they were filled with wet cement, and there was a rushing sound in her ears.

How had he known? She'd never told anyone that the alcohol Tyler consumed that night had turned him into a stranger. Someone who'd turned on her—who'd *hurt* her—when she'd said no to his advances. But somehow, Matt had guessed the truth.

"Zoey?" Rose took a tentative forward, and Zoey's heart went out to the woman when she saw the shattered look on her face.

"I'm sorry," Rose mumbled. "I hope…someday you can forgive me for holding a grudge all these years."

Zoey's throat tightened, making it difficult to breathe. "How about right now?"

Rose bit her lip, as if she didn't quite believe forgiveness could be offered so freely.

Zoey understood. It had taken her a long time to accept God's forgiveness. And to forgive herself.

She spotted Delia and Morgan standing near the old piano in the corner and suddenly knew what to do.

"Usually the choir performs a song from the cantata," she said. "Tonight we're going to do something different." Zoey saw Delia's eyebrows disappear under the brim of her straw hat and gave her a reassuring wink. "We're all going to sing one of the songs together."

She sat down on the rickety piano bench and took a deep breath. And started to play "Amazing Grace."

One by one, everyone pushed closer.

Tears blurred Zoey's eyes as Gran and her parents joined in. She felt Matt's hand rest on her shoulder, and the promise lingered in the warmth of his touch.

As the chorus ended, the air felt lighter. Conversation and soft ripples of laughter stirred the air as everyone made their way to the tables laden with food.

Kate paused and looked back at Zoey and Matt, a mischievous grin on her face. "So, Zoey, does this mean you're looking forward to tomorrow?"

Zoey glanced at Matt. What she saw in his eyes both terrified her and filled her with joy. "Yes," she whispered. "I think I am."

* * *

"Looks like we're done here, Pastor." Daniel Red-stone tucked the last of the folding tables away in the oversize storage closet off the fellowship room. "Do you want me to lock up for the night?"

"I can do it." Matt's gaze swept around the room. Most of the people who'd attended the potluck had left already. The last few volunteers on the cleanup crew had finished straightening up the kitchen and drifted out, the low murmur of their voices echoing in the stairwell.

But where was Zoey?

Matt knew she hadn't left with her parents. Liz had gotten tired, so Paul and Sara Decker had taken her home shortly after the meal ended. Zoey remained to check on some last-minute details for the cantata. Matt had seen her talking to Haylie and Rob, but there was no sign of the teens now. And no sign of Zoey, either.

Matt shut the lights off and made his way upstairs, determined not to let another moment go by without telling Zoey how he felt about her. And find out how she felt about *him*.

A sliver of light shining beneath the doors of the sanctuary caught his eye.

He should have known.

Matt pushed open the door. Zoey remained silent as he sat down on the pew beside her, so close their shoulders were almost touching.

For a moment, neither of them spoke.

"How did you know?" Zoey finally asked. "About... Tyler?"

"I heard what you told me—and what you didn't," Matt said simply. The police report Jake Sutton provided had only verified his suspicions.

"I didn't think anyone would believe me. And I...I couldn't help but feel that it was my fault," Zoey murmured. "I left with Tyler willingly. I knew he'd been drinking."

"You were a victim," Matt struggled to keep his voice even as he pictured Zoey the night of the accident, scared and hurting. "It was time the truth came out."

"Not everyone will believe it." Zoey shifted away from him and Matt felt a moment of gut-wrenching fear.

After everything that had happened, did she still think that her past would always cast a shadow over them? Hadn't she realized that the things she'd gone through had forged her character—had made her into the only woman he wanted by his side?

"I can't change people's attitudes or their hearts, but God can," Matt said, silently praying for the right words to say. The words that would convince Zoey that he wanted her to be part of his life. "I trust Him."

"But—"

Matt put a finger against her lips. Maybe the words weren't so hard to find, after all. "I trust God...and I love you."

Zoey stared at him, wide-eyed. It was what she'd been afraid of—yet longed to—hear. A lump formed in her throat, making it difficult to breathe.

"I love you, Zoey," Matt repeated.

Zoey shot to her feet. "How can you?"

"How can I *not?*" Matt countered softly. "Sometimes I wondered who—if anyone—God had in mind for me. You don't know how many times members of my congregation tried to set me up on blind dates with someone they claimed was "perfect." No one ever was. Until I met you."

"But that's just it." Zoey closed her eyes. "I'm *not* perfect."

"You're perfect for me." Matt's hand cupped her chin, and he gently forced her to look at him. "That's what matters."

Zoey wanted to believe it. Matt had boldly faced some of her accusers and told them the truth about what had happened with Tyler that night, but she also knew that some people would never forget her rebellion and the heartache she'd caused her family.

"I don't want to damage your reputation. Everyone wants their perfect pastor to find the perfect wife."

A shadow passed over Matt's face. "This pastor is far from perfect, Zoey. There are things in my past that I never had the courage to tell people about because I was afraid I might lose their respect. I didn't realize that if I was honest about my mistakes, if I could share how God had forgiven and healed me, it would encourage people who had gone through the same thing. You showed me that."

"Me?"

"Yes, you. I told you that you're a wise woman. Wise and sweet and strong." Matt gave her a lopsided smile. "To be honest, I wonder if I'm good enough for *you*."

The glint of laughter in Matt's eyes told Zoey that he was teasing, but she also saw a flicker of uncertainty. He'd shared his heart—confessed that he loved her. But instead of throwing herself into his arms—which was what she'd wanted to do—she had retreated behind her doubts once again.

It was time to follow Matt's example. To put her trust in God and open her heart to the man He had brought into her life.

Zoey let out the breath she'd been holding. "I love you, too, Matt."

He froze. "What did you say?"

"I love you, Matt. I—" Zoey forgot what she'd been about to say as Matt drew her into his arms. Slowly, carefully, as if she were something precious. They fit together perfectly—two halves of a whole.

"One more time." Matt demanded, his voice unsteady.

Zoey's hand lifted to cradle his firm jaw. "I love you."

"Zoey…" Matt drew in a ragged breath. In his eyes, Zoey saw the promise of a future. Their future. Then he bent his head and his lips met hers in a kiss that was sweeter than the first—and shattered the last of her remaining doubts and fears.

"I guess that means you believe me," Zoey gasped when they finally broke apart.

Matt smiled down at her.

"I believe in us."

Epilogue

"You again."

Matt handed his ticket to Brit and pointed to the gold crown in the corner. "I need my tux."

Hiding a grin, the young woman snapped her gum and pivoted on tangerine stilettos. "Follow me."

Matt caught a glimpse of Melissa further down the hallway. She cast a furtive glance over her shoulder and gave him a thumbs-up sign.

The rest of the cast knew he was here, but Zoey didn't.

Over the past three months, his responsibilities at church made it difficult to travel to Lake Delton, but Zoey assured him that she looked forward to driving to Mirror Lake whenever her schedule allowed.

A long-distance relationship had proved to be more challenging than Matt would have thought possible. For both of them.

This time, Matt wanted to surprise her.

"Time to make the switch." Mike, the assistant

director, pulled a red velvet box out of his pocket and handed it to Matt. Brit smiled in approval as he replaced the plastic ring inside with the simple, marquis cut diamond he had purchased the week before.

"You're on in five, dude." Mike slapped him on the back.

Brit helped him into the tux and opened the door. "Break a leg."

Through a gap in the curtain, Matt saw Zoey kneeling on the stage in her tattered jeans and pink high-top tennies.

"Where's my script?" he whispered to the stage-hand.

A kid who wasn't a whole lot older than Zach Davis handed it over. "Are you going to follow it this time?"

Matt grinned. "Absolutely not."

"What are you doing here?" Zoey almost collapsed face-first into the blue confetti when she saw Matt standing in front of her.

He winked at her. "Surprise."

That, Zoey thought, was an understatement.

She hadn't expected to see Matt until the following day, when she drove to Mirror Lake for the weekend.

Not that she was complaining.

The truth was, it was getting more and more difficult to leave him.

She took a deep breath, gave him a meaningful

"I'll-deal-with-you-later" look and became Ella Cinders for the next forty-five minutes.

During Melissa's solo, Zoey zipped into the back room for the last wardrobe change. Brit helped her into the ball gown.

Zoey heard her sniffle.

"Are you crying?" she asked in astonishment.

"No." Brit sniffled again. "Allergies. Now get out of here."

Zoey walked back on stage and heard the audience gasp. The ball gown had that effect on people. Matt was waiting for her in the middle of the stage, drop dead gorgeous in his borrowed tux.

She glided up to him.

"Zoey..."

Oops. He'd broken character. She hid a smile.

"It's Ella," one of the extras, a teenage boy who had been flexing his acting muscles throughout the performance, whispered.

Matt passed the clipboard to one of Zoey's "stepsisters" before taking her hand. "I love you, Zoey."

Zoey almost choked on the lump that swelled in her throat.

"Ella," the teenager reminded Matt.

The three women sitting at the table closest to the stage shushed him.

Matt's eyes lit with laughter and Zoey clapped a hand over her mouth. Matt gently drew it away. Holding it tight, he went down on one knee and removed the ring from his pocket.

There was absolute silence in the audience, as if everyone was beginning to realize this wasn't part of the script.

"I want you beside me, Zoey. Loving me and laughing with me. I want us to grow together and make mistakes together." The hazel eyes glowed with a gentle fire. "I had a feeling that meeting you was part of God's plan. Now I'm sure. He planned on *us*." Zoey felt Matt's fingers tremble. "Will you marry me?"

Zoey started to cry. "Yes. *Yes*."

Matt slid the ring on her finger—a perfect fit.

She became dimly aware that the audience was on its feet. People were applauding. And whistling.

Some of the extras looked down at the scripts and then at Matt and Zoey again.

"You're supposed to sweep her off her feet," The kid muttered, rolling his eyes at Matt's incompetence.

Zoey heard him and grinned. "He already did."

"Some things," Matt said softly. "Deserve a repeat performance."

Before Zoey knew it, Matt had captured her in the circle of his arms. Lifted her off her feet.

"Come home with me? For good this time?" he murmured against her hair.

The words sweetened Zoey's soul. She wrapped her arms around Matt's neck and pressed her face against his heart.

"I am home."

* * * * *

Dear Reader,

I hope you enjoyed your third visit to Mirror Lake! Writing Matt and Zoey's story reminded me how often we tend to let the past color the future—whether our own or someone else's. I'm so thankful that God has the power to change hearts and lives. He really does give us a new song to sing! Don't forget that someone needs to hear yours.

Please watch for the next book in the MIRROR LAKE series, when small-town girl Kate Nichols finally meets her match!

I love to hear from my readers. Please visit my website at www.kathrynspringer.com and say hello.

Blessings,

Kathryn Springer

QUESTIONS FOR DISCUSSION

1. In the opening scene of the book, Zoey remembers the adage "you can't go home again." What do you think that means? Do you think it is true? Why or why not?

2. What was Matt Wilde's first impression of Zoey? What was that impression based on? Describe a time when you misjudged someone—or when someone misjudged you—the first time you met.

3. Can you draw any parallels between Zoey's return to Mirror Lake and the parable of the prodigal son? What are they?

4. Why does Zoey fight her attraction to Matt? Do you think her underlying concerns are valid? Why or why not?

5. Have you or someone you love ever been the target of gossip? What were the circumstances? How did you feel?

6. Expectations can cause conflict in relationships. In what way? How was this true for Zoey?

7. Both Matt and Zoey had things in their past

they weren't proud of. How did this affect their perception of themselves? Their perception of God?

8. Read Psalm 40. Which verses speak to you the most? Why?

9. In spite of her initial resistance, Zoey agrees to direct the cantata. Why? Have you ever done something "outside your comfort zone"? What was it?

10. Why did Zoey believe that she could never be a suitable wife for Matt?

11. 2 Corinthians 1:4 says "(the God of all comfort), who comforts us in all our troubles, so that we can comfort those in any trouble with the comfort we ourselves received from God." What did this passage mean to Zoey? What does it mean to you?

12. Zoey was able to use her past experiences to encourage Haylie, another girl who had a "reputation" and who'd made some mistakes. Have you ever shared your story to encourage someone?

13. What was your favorite scene? Why?

14. Zoey and her parents reconcile near the end of the book. Do you think it will be easy for them to move forward? Why or why not? What role will forgiveness have to play?

15. Zoey loves Matt, but she was afraid her past would get in the way of their future. Do you think those fears were valid? How did Matt finally convince Zoey that they were meant to be together?

LARGER-PRINT BOOKS!

**GET 2 FREE
LARGER-PRINT NOVELS
PLUS 2 FREE
MYSTERY GIFTS**

Love Inspired®

Larger-print novels are now available...

YES! Please send me 2 FREE LARGER-PRINT Love Inspired® novels and my 2 FREE mystery gifts (gifts are worth about $10). After receiving them, if I don't wish to receive any more books, I can return the shipping statement marked "cancel". If I don't cancel, I will receive 6 brand-new novels every month and be billed just $4.74 per book in the U.S. or $5.24 per book in Canada. That's a saving of at least 24% off the cover price. It's quite a bargain! Shipping and handling is just 50¢ per book in the U.S. and 75¢ per book in Canada.* I understand that accepting the 2 free books and gifts places me under no obligation to buy anything. I can always return a shipment and cancel at any time. Even if I never buy another book, the two free books and gifts are mine to keep forever.

122/322 IDN FC79

Name _____ (PLEASE PRINT) _____

Address _____ Apt. # _____

City _____ State/Prov. _____ Zip/Postal Code _____

Signature (if under 18, a parent or guardian must sign)

Mail to the **Reader Service:**
IN U.S.A.: P.O. Box 1867, Buffalo, NY 14240-1867
IN CANADA: P.O. Box 609, Fort Erie, Ontario L2A 5X3

Not valid to current subscribers to Love Inspired Larger-Print books.

**Are you a current subscriber to Love Inspired books
and want to receive the larger-print edition?
Call 1-800-873-8635 or visit www.ReaderService.com.**

* Terms and prices subject to change without notice. Prices do not include applicable taxes. Sales tax applicable in N.Y. Canadian residents will be charged applicable taxes. Offer not valid in Quebec. This offer is limited to one order per household. All orders subject to credit approval. Credit or debit balances in a customer's account(s) may be offset by any other outstanding balance owed by or to the customer. Please allow 4 to 6 weeks for delivery. Offer available while quantities last.

Your Privacy—The Reader Service is committed to protecting your privacy. Our Privacy Policy is available online at www.ReaderService.com or upon request from the Reader Service.

We make a portion of our mailing list available to reputable third parties that offer products we believe may interest you. If you prefer that we not exchange your name with third parties, or if you wish to clarify or modify your communication preferences, please visit us at www.ReaderService.com/consumerchoice or write to us at Reader Service Preference Service, P.O. Box 9062, Buffalo, NY 14269. Include your complete name and address.

LILPI I